FOCUS

A collection of multi-cultural stories for assembly

6

6

Focus

A collection of

Bell & Hyman

London

Published in 1983 by
BELL & HYMAN LIMITED
Denmark House
37–39 Queen Elizabeth Street
London SE1 2QB

British Library Cataloguing in Publication Data
Brandling, Redvers
    Focus: a collection of multi-cultural stories for assembly.
    I. Title.
    823′.914[J] PZ7

ISBN 0 237 29335 8

Phototypeset by Tradespools Limited, Frome, Somerset
Printed in Great Britain by Spottiswoode Ballantyne Ltd,
Colchester and London

INTRODUCTION

For hundreds of years the heritage of various ethnic groups was preserved by stories which were told by one generation to the next. Eventually many of these stories came to be written down and, when this was done, an enormous, multi-cultural literary 'bank' was established. The currency in this bank concerns themes such as courage, duty, faith, humour, friendship, foolishness, injustice, joy, mystery, values, waste and wisdom. In short it is a depository from which the presenters of assemblies may draw with great advantage.

This book seeks to present a selection of these stories, and its title is derived from a consideration of how they might be used to greatest effect. The following flow chart suggests an approach:

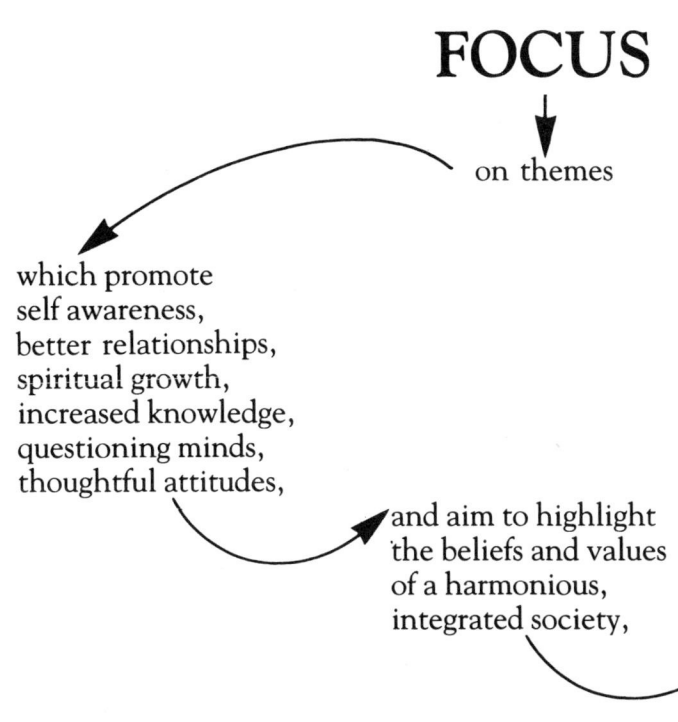

FOCUS

on themes

which promote
self awareness,
better relationships,
spiritual growth,
increased knowledge,
questioning minds,
thoughtful attitudes,

and aim to highlight
the beliefs and values
of a harmonious,
integrated society,

by means of
a wide variety of
stories from multi-
cultural backgrounds
and from resources
which include folk
tales, reported
stories of contemporary
life, mystery,
fiction and poetry.

Following on from this flow-chart it seems necessary to establish the themes in more detail, and then link various groups of stories, passages and poems to each theme. Thus:

Group 1   contains material which seeks to aid self awareness by considering values such as truth and love.

Group 2   contains that which seeks to promote a consideration of better relationships via stories about the virtues of decency, honesty, self sacrifice, courage, friendship, forgiveness, awareness of one's own limitations.

Group 3   contains that which may promote spiritual growth via wonder at the marvels of the world, awe in the presence of the unknown, majesty and mystery and other people's interpretation of these.

Group 4   contains that which may increase knowledge by speculation about human nature with due regard to all its frailties and failures.

Group 5   contains that which stimulates questioning minds via sympathy for the deprived and unfortunate, anger at cruelty and exploitation, and respect for those who rise above it.

Group 6   contains that which provokes thoughtful attitudes about the delight of being alive.

The practical arrangement of the book is therefore of one hundred and two items divided into six groups. It is hoped however that this will not lead to any inflexibility—many teachers will want to use stories and poems in different contexts, bearing in mind the specific needs of their groups of children.

In my experience stories used in assembly are best read in advance, assimilated and then 're-told'. All of those in this book are short enough for this approach, but an attempt has been made to adapt them specially for 'reading aloud' if this is preferred.

Acknowledgements

I am grateful to many people for their help with this book. As always the staff and children of Dewhurst St. Mary School, Chestnut, Herts. have been both an inspiration and a never ending source of material. Individuals from whom I have heard stories or been guided to sources, and to whom I owe a great debt, are Canon R.O. Osborne, Pat Garrett, Julia Stanton of Evans Brothers, Maurice Lynch of the West London Institute of Higher Education, and Miss M.T. Vakatale, Deputy High Commissioner, Fiji High Commission.

Other help and advice regarding sources and material has been given by Anna Girvan, Librarian, United States Embassy; Miss M. Williams of the Barbadian High Commission; Clive Lawton, Education Officer of the Board of Deputies of British Jews; the librarian at the Sri Lankan High Commission in London; the Jamaican and Malaysian High Commissions.

The compiler of any anthology like this must inevitably be something of a plagiarist. I have consulted many and varied sources and found numerous stories duplicated in slightly altered forms in different cultures. Every effort has been made to establish the copyright holders of the material used. Where these efforts have been unsuccessful the author and publishers would be pleased to hear from copyright holders.

For those teachers who would like to consider a greater selection of stories from some of the cultures referred to in this book, then the following material is recommended.

Tales Told near a Crocodile, H. Harman, Hutchinson
Stories Told round the World, Taya Zinkin, O.U.P.
The Ivory City, Marcus Crouch, Granada
The Caravan of Dreams, Idris Shah, Octagon Press
Gods and Men, J. Bailey, K. McLeish, D. Spearman, O.U.P.
Indian Village Tales, Prafulla Mohanti, Davis Poynter
My World, Michael Pollard, Macdonald Educ. in association with United
    Nations Children's Fund
Dragons, Gods and Spirits from Chinese Mythology, T.T.L. Sanders, Peter Lowe
Why the Hyena Does Not Care for Fish, Peggy Appiah, André Deutsch
Coyote the Trickster, G. Robinson, D. Hill, Chatto and Windus
Tales from the Panchantantra, L. Clarke, Evans
Fables, A. Lobel, Jonathan Cape
Fables from La Fontaine, K. Muggeridge, William Collins
Tales from the South Pacific Islands, Anne Gittins, Stemmer House
Armenian Folk Tales and Fables, C. Downing, O.U.P.
Tales from Australia, S. Coulden, W.H. Allen

CONTENTS

Group 5

Group 6

1. The Precious Stone

The king was very old and he decided that he must share out the royal treasure. He had two sons and one daughter. The sons were called Prince Hongse Yout, who was the oldest, and Prince Hongse Noi.

'Hmm,' thought the old king. 'Prince Hongse Yout is my oldest son so he must get the great emerald.'

Now the great emerald was a stone so precious that it was worth far more than all the rest of the king's wealth put together. When Prince Hongse Noi heard that his brother was to get it he was angry.

'Father,' he said, 'what you are giving me is nothing compared to what you are giving my brother. We should share the emerald.'

'Father,' said the king's daughter, 'what you are giving me is nothing at all.'

'Father,' said Prince Hongse Yout, 'what a wise man you are. It is quite right that I should have the great emerald because I am the oldest son.'

So great arguments broke out in the palace. Some of the king's relatives thought he was being wise, others thought he was being unfair. Each of the princes had people arguing for them and a few even argued for the princess. For weeks there was talk of nothing but the great emerald and who should get it. Then one night it was stolen and nobody ever saw it again.

adapted from *Folk Tales of Thailand* by P.C.R. Chandhur

2. If

IF only.
IF only I could.
IF I were I would.
IF ever I did,
IF ever I do.
Surely this word IF has the
biggest meaning of any other
Two-letter word.
IF only I knew how
IF only I knew why
IF ever I found out
IF ever I could find out.
Would I?
I would like to,
but would I?
IF a person asked me to explain
what IF means, would I dare?
say anything?
The word IF could have a
meaning which no other person
has yet! thought of.
IF IF IF

IF I were a rich man would I?
And IF I were a poor man, would I?
IF neither?
IF I were a middle-class man I
would, surely,
Wouldn't I?
IF I only knew
If only!
IF I only could
IF I were I would
IF ever I did,
IF ever I do,
IF only I knew how.
IF only I knew why.
IF ever I found out.
IF ever I could find out.
IF ever I could find out
Would I?
IF IF IF . . .

Charlie Savvides

3. The Boy Who Forgot His Mother

Malin Kundang and his mother were very poor indeed. They lived in a small hut, never had enough food and dressed in clothes that were little better than rags.

'This is no good,' said the mother when her son was fifteen years old. 'You will be able to do far better if you don't have me to bother about. Go my son, leave me here and see if you can make your fortune in the world. Perhaps, if you are successful you might come back to see me some time.'

'But mother . . .' began Malin Kundang.

'No buts,' said his mother. 'Take what rice we have and go.'

So Malin Kundang left his poor mother and soon got a job on one of the boats which carried goods and food up and down the great river. Now it so happened that he was a very good worker and the man who owned the boat had no children of his own.

'I like Malin Kundang,' said the owner of the boat to himself. 'I wish I'd had a son like him. Well . . . why don't I adopt him as my son?'

The boat owner did this and soon they were able to buy another boat, and then another. When the old man died all the boats were left to Malin Kundang and he was now a very rich man indeed.

Of course the people of his town heard about his success and his mother was very pleased for him—although she did wish he would come and see her. Then one day one of Malin Kundang's boats had some business in his old town and he was on board when it stopped there.

There was a lot of excitement when people heard this and everybody started saying 'Malin Kundang pulang' which means 'Malin Kundang is returning'. Naturally his mother heard this.

She gathered together a little rice in her cooking pot and went to meet her son. She was still terribly poor and the rice was all she had but she so much wanted to give her son something.

When she got to his fine ship she asked to see him, but one of the crew, looking at the old lady in rags said, 'His mother? You look more like a beggar to me. Be off with you.'

Then Malin Kundang appeared on deck and pushing past the rest of the crew his mother rushed to greet him.

'Malin Kundang, it's me—your mother. How pleased I am that you have done so well. I've brought you a small present.'

Malin Kundang saw all his men looking at the old ragged woman, then he looked down at his own fine clothes. He saw the old bowl with the dried up rice in it . . .

'Get this woman off my ship,' he shouted.

'But my son . . .'

The crew grabbed Malin Kundang's mother and threw her ashore. The pot of rice which she had brought to give to her son fell into the river and sank.

At that moment the sky clouded over, there was a terrific clap of thunder and a fork of lightning shot from the sky and hit the boat. With a crash it turned over and sank immediately, taking all on board with it.

The next morning, on the spot where the boat had sunk, a mysterious rock had appeared. It stayed there to remind everybody of the story of Malin Kundang and his mother.

adapted from *Folk Tales of Indonesia* by A. Soebiantoro and M. Ratnatunga

4. A Fair Exchange

There was once a brahman who was a very good man. He helped others as much as he could; he prayed often, but he was very poor. His wife and children often did not have enough to eat. The brahman worried about this and often mentioned it in his prayers.

One day he was praying when Durga and her husband, the great god Shiva, heard him.

'Poor fellow,' said Shiva, 'we must do something to help him. Let him have a pot.'

So, as the brahman opened his eyes, he saw the goddess Durga standing over him. Beside her was a cooking pot.

'Your prayers have been answered, brahman,' she said. 'Whenever you want anything to eat just tip this pot up and out will come your fill of rice.'

'Thank you, thank you,' said the brahman, and the goddess disappeared. The brahman tipped up the pot and sure enough a stream of rice came out. Putting this into a little bundle he hurried off with his pot.

It was a long way to his home, and very hot. When he passed an inn which had a large water tank for washing he stopped.

'Could I use some water to get washed with please?' asked the brahman, and when the innkeeper nodded he went on:

'Please look after this pot while I am washing. It is very, very precious so please take great care of it.'

When he was washing the innkeeper looked at the pot.

'What could he have that is precious?' murmured the innkeeper to himself. 'This looks an ordinary old pot to me.'

As he spoke he turned the pot upside down, and out came the rice. Getting a shock at this, the innkeeper turned the pot upside down again, and again.

'Now I know why it is so precious,' he thought. 'I must do something about this.'

So he quickly searched his kitchen until he found a pot which looked exactly the same. Changing the pots round he gave the brahman the kitchen pot when he came back.

'Thank you,' said the brahman and hurried off to tell his family his good news. Of course this time the pot produced nothing and the brahman was very upset to see the disappointment of his wife and children. When he thought about it he decided that the innkeeper must have tricked him in some way.

That night he prayed again and when Durga heard him she was annoyed that he had lost his pot so easily but she was even more annoyed with the innkeeper. When the brahman stopped praying he found another pot beside him.

Joyfully turning it over he was shocked when out leapt a bunch of evil spirits who leapt on him and gave him a beating. Desperately he grappled for the pot and turned it back. The evil spirits disappeared inside it.

'Ha,' said Durga, who was watching, 'that will have taught him not to be so careless with his gifts. I wonder what he'll do now.'

What the brahman did next was to head straight for the inn again, and tell the innkeeper the same story as before.

'This man is a fool,' thought the innkeeper when the brahman had gone to wash. 'I wonder what treasures this pot holds.'

Turning the pot upside down, he then staggered back as the creatures poured out and attacked him. They then began to tear his house to pieces—until the brahman returned and righted the pot.

The innkeeper had not only been shocked, he had learned his lesson too. Hurrying off he brought back the first pot, gave it to the brahman and apologised for his theft.

So the brahman hurried off home, and he and his family lived in happiness and plenty for the rest of their lives.

5. The Good Sons

Once, a farmer died and left what he had to his two sons. He left all his corn tied up in bags. Half of it was put on one side of a barn, half of it was put on the other side.

Anwar, one of the brothers, went to bed that night and lay awake for a long time.

'It is sad my father is no longer with us,' he thought. 'I wonder too if he thought enough about my brother. After all I have no wife or children to look after and my brother has. He needs our father's wealth much more than I do. I'll just creep down to the barn and drag some of my sacks over onto his side.'

So Anwar crept down to the barn and dragged some of his sacks over to his brother's pile. When he had finished he went back to bed.

Now Omar, the other brother, couldn't sleep either. He got up out of bed and he looked at the moonlight streaming into the bedroom. It shone on the peaceful face of his wife as she lay there asleep. Then Omar went into the other bedrooms and looked at his children who were all sleeping soundly.

'Hmm,' thought Omar, 'I wish our father had left more of his wealth to Anwar. After all I am lucky enough to have my wife and children but Anwar has neither. I must do something about it.'

So Omar crept down to the barn—in fact he just missed Anwar who was on his way back to bed. When he reached the barn Omar dragged some sacks from his pile and put them beside Anwar's. When he had finished he went back to bed.

Next morning when the two brothers went to the barn they couldn't believe their eyes. Each still had the same number of sacks he had had the day before.

adapted from *The Caravan of Dreams* by I. Shah

6.   Show A Good Example

One day Mohammed was in a town when he saw a lot of people walking towards him.

'Where do they come from?' he asked.

'Oh, they come from Mudar,' said one of his friends.

'But just look at them,' said Mohammed.

Then everybody looked at the people from Mudar. They were a very sad sight. There wasn't one of them who was dressed in proper clothes, all of them looked half starved, and there were only a few left who had swords hanging round their backs.

Mohammed was angry.

'Well, what is this town going to do about these people?' he asked in a loud voice.

Several people looked away, but not one man. He went straight to his house and came back with more money than he could carry in two hands. He began to give it to the poor people of Mudar. When his friends saw this they too quietly went off to their own houses. Soon they were back with money, food and clothes. They gave these away.

As Mohammed watched this he smiled.

'You know,' he said to his friends. 'If one person starts to do something good his reward is that other people will follow him in doing good things too.'

7. Do Not Be Too Proud

Aliya was the daughter of a very rich merchant and she had six sisters. Now the merchant was one of those people who liked others to tell him what a good and clever man he was.

One day he asked all his daughters some questions.

'Who looks after you? Who sees that you are happy? Whom do you depend on?'

All his daughters, except Aliya, said, 'You father,' and the merchant smiled at his own goodness. But when Aliya was asked the question, she said: 'I depend on myself.'

The merchant was furious. Without bothering to ask Aliya what she really meant he began to shout and rave at her. Finally he told her to get out of his house altogether. What's more he wouldn't allow her to take any money or any food.

Sadly Aliya left the house but as she did so her old nurse saw her.

'Where are you going Aliya?' she asked.

When Aliya told her the story she was shocked.

'Well, if that's the case then I am going to come with you,' said the nurse. So the two of them left the fine house and went out into the jungle.

By the time it was almost night they were in the depths of the jungle and were very frightened. Then a tree spoke to them.

'If you stay out there when the animals are searching for their food this evening you won't live long. Squeeze into this hollow part of my trunk and you will be safe.'

So Aliya and her nurse spent an uncomfortable and frightening night, but at least they were saved from hunting animals.

The next day they found a market in a city. All they had between them was five shells but they managed to exchange these for some rice. Taking the rice back to their friendly tree they ate some of it, scattered the rest on the ground nearby and then got into their hollow for the night.

Whilst they were asleep some peacocks, looking for food, found the rice. They were so greedy that they fought over it. The next morning when Aliya looked out she saw that the ground was covered with beautiful feathers which had been torn out in the fighting.

With the feathers, Aliya and the nurse made some beautiful fans and sold them at the market. With some of the money they got they bought more rice to scatter and so got more feathers. Soon, because they were clever and worked hard, they became quite rich.

Thanking the tree for all his kindness they left and arranged for some men to build them a fine house. One day Aliya was watching the work when she saw a man and a woman sweating in the hot sun whilst they dug a deep hole in the ground so that a water tank could be put in it. As she looked she saw, to her astonishment, that the two were her mother and father! She asked a servant to bring them to her.

Now after Aliya had left home the merchant had fallen on hard times and lost all his money. He and his wife had been wandering round looking for any kind of work when they had seen the building going on. They had got work then as labourers. So, when they were sent for, they were very frightened because they knew that it was a custom to kill workers and bury their bodies in the foundations of great houses.

As they followed the servant they were even more afraid when he said, 'You are to wash thoroughly and put on these fine clothes.'

Then, they were brought before Aliya. Speechless, they saw that it was the daughter they had cruelly ordered out of their home. Aliya, however, held out her arms to them to show that all was forgiven.

Her father, who had missed his daughter very much indeed, wept with joy at seeing her again.

'You were right,' he said, 'to depend on yourself.'

After a joyful meal Aliya gave her father a large sum of money so that he could become a prosperous merchant again.

adapted from *The Ivory City* by M. Crouch

8. What Is Clever?

When Peter was a boy all the other children laughed at him. He always seemed to be the child who tripped over or upset the paints or made a mess of his work. Now Peter didn't like this but no matter how hard he tried he didn't seem to be able to do things any better.

As he grew older he worked on his mother's farm and he became big and strong. He worked very hard and he was always kind and friendly, but he still wished he was cleverer.

'I know what I'll do,' he said to himself one day. 'I'll go and see that old woman who everybody says is a witch. She might help me.'

This took a lot of courage because everybody was frightened of the strange old woman who lived in a cottage deep in the woods.

However Peter went to her cottage one day after work. It was already getting dark when he reached the cottage and he felt very nervous as he knocked on the door. A sharp voice told him to come in and when he did so he found himself looking into an old lined face from which two eyes shone fiercely.

'Well?' said the old woman in the same sharp voice. Nervously Peter explained to her that he wanted to be clever.

When she heard what he had to say the old woman spoke again.

'Before I can do anything you will have to answer a riddle.'

'Yes,' said Peter.

'What runs without legs?'

Peter stared blankly. He tried to think of an answer—any answer. Nothing came into his mind.

'I don't know,' he muttered.

'In that case,' replied the old woman, 'Go away'.

Peter went miserably home. Next day he thought he would try again. Plucking up all his courage he went back along the dark, overgrown path to the dingy cottage.

'So you're back,' said the old woman when he was inside again.

'Yes . . . will you give me another chance . . . please?'

'All right. What is yellow, shines—but is not gold?'

Again Peter thought desperately. Nothing came into his mind. Finally, not daring to admit that he couldn't work this out either he dashed out of the cottage and stumbled through the wood.

'Oh dear, I'll never be clever,' he murmured to himself and slumped down on a tree stump beside a river. Presently a beautiful girl came along and Peter and she soon got talking to each other.

Peter found the girl, whose name was Jenny, wonderfully easy to talk to. When he went home he arranged to meet her again. They met again—and again—and soon decided that they would like to marry each other.

Everyone was very surprised at this, but Peter was so kind and hard working that he made a very good husband. Jenny helped him run the farm and they were very happy.

Then one day Peter got to thinking as he worked in the fields.

'If only I were clever. Jenny is so good to me, I'd like to be cleverer for her sake.'

When he got home that night he told Jenny about the old woman in the cottage.

'All right,' said Jenny, 'if you want to go again let's go together.'

So once again Peter found himself in the old woman's cottage.

'Oh so it's you,' she said. 'You've probably even forgotten the questions I asked you so I'll give them to you again. What runs without legs?'

Again Peter found himself thinking desperately, but Jenny called out immediately, 'A river.'

'Hmm,' said the old woman, 'and what is yellow, shines but is not gold?'

'Oh, the sun of course,' said Jenny.

'Let's give you one more then,' said the old woman. 'What starts with no legs, but soon has two and then four?'

Quick as a flash Jenny answered, 'A tadpole,'

The old woman then turned and looked at Peter and Jenny.

'And what was it you wanted young man?' she said to Peter.

'To be clever,' mumbled Peter.

'You've been clever enough to marry such a beautiful and clever wife—and make her happy by the look of it. Now, don't waste my time—go home and enjoy your good fortune.'

So Peter and Jenny went home and lived happily for the rest of their days.

9. What We Think We See

When Nasrudin became fifteen years of age he determined to see something of the world. There was an old saying at that time: 'Seek knowledge even if it be in China.'

So Nasrudin set off on his donkey. He travelled through deserts and mountains, staying in many different places and meeting many people. He learnt a great deal and after almost twelve years he was still journeying, this time through the mountains of Kashmir.

'This is one of the most difficult trips yet,' said Nasrudin to his faithful donkey as they climbed high into the thin air. Then the traveller looked again at his donkey who seemed suddenly to be slowing down.

'What is . . .'

Before Nasrudin could finish speaking the donkey fell to the ground and died. It had finally become exhausted with old age and ceaseless travel.

Nasrudin fell on his knees beside the creature and wept bitterly. In all the years of his journeys the donkey had been his faithful companion and friend. Now he was dead.

Nasrudin dug a grave, buried the donkey and left a simple mound of earth to mark the spot. Then, he found that he had lost his desire to go on. He stayed in the beautiful mountain scenery, caring for the grave.

Now the road on which he had been travelling was quite a busy one and travellers passed by regularly. As they did so they noticed Nasrudin and began to talk about him.

'That must have been a dear friend who died there.'

'Yes, I think it must have been someone important too.'

'Why is that?'

'Well look how long that man has stayed to look after the grave and mourn his loss.'

'I wouldn't be surprised if it was a holy man who died there and that this is his disciple.'

So the talk went on, whilst Nasrudin said nothing. One day a very rich man came by. He had heard the stories of the man on the mountainside and when he saw the grave he came to a decision.

'That grave must belong to a very important holy man,' he thought. 'Such a person should have a proper shrine to mark where he lies.'

So the rich man gave orders for a huge shrine with a large impressive dome to be erected over the mound grave. When this was finished it needed money spending on it to keep it in good repair. Other men then made terraces on the hillside. On these terraces crops were grown and the money made from their sale went for the caring of the shrine. The fame of the great burial place, and the silent man who stayed there, spread far and wide.

10. Sudden Help

There are times when most of us need help quickly and urgently. Because these situations are usually unexpected we may find that the help comes from somebody we have never even met.

Jack was studying for an examination. It was late at night and his exam was early the next morning. Jack sat in his bedroom with his books spread out in front of him. He was trying desperately to remember the facts but all the time the noise thumped in his head.

Jack's parents were having a party. In fact they often had parties and weren't really bothered about Jack's studies. Night after night the noise and music went on into the early hours and Jack could neither work nor sleep.

Suddenly he could stand it no longer. Bursting from his room he leapt down the stairs and barged out through the front door. His father saw him and ran shouting after.

Jack knew it was no good trying to explain yet again. There'd been so many rows and things never got any better. With his shirt flapping in the night wind he ran and ran. Then, breathless, he stopped. Where was he going? Who could help? If he couldn't work at home where could he work!

It was then that he saw the telephone box. As he did so he remembered a notice he had seen recently. It had said, 'Desperate?—Ring the Samaritans.'

Thankfully feeling some loose change in his trouser pocket Jack went into the telephone kiosk, looked up the number of the local Samaritans and dialled.

There was a click as the connection was made and a voice spoke into Jack's ear.

'This is the Samaritans, can I help you?'

'I'm desperate,' said Jack, 'Can you help?'

'I'll try,' replied the voice, 'can you tell me quickly what the trouble is?'

It took only seconds for Jack to say that he had ran away from home and had an important exam in the morning.

'Right,' said the voice at the other end. 'Don't waste any more time talking there. Come round now and we'll talk.'

When Jack heard the man at the other end of the line give an address he was surprised that it was very near.

'I can be there within a few minutes,' he said.

So Jack met Chuck, the Samaritan who he had spoken to on the telephone. Jack was amazed that Chuck was prepared to ask him round in the middle of the night, to give him a warm drink and listen sympathetically to his troubles.

But Chuck was to do much more than this. He was able to give Jack the support he needed to get his life sorted out once and for all. One telephone call had provided sudden—and lasting help.

11. The Wise Ruler

There was once a man called Amin. He and his wife Nazira were greedy. They weren't greedy for food or clothes or possessions—just gold. Each day they spent as little as possible on food so that they could hoard more money. Each day their clothes grew older and more ragged. Each night they got out their money bags and counted their treasure.

Now Amin was a servant for a great and powerful Caliph who was known by all as a wise and fair man. One day when Amin was at work Nazira went shopping at the market. As usual she looked for the cheapest food she could buy—and then she had a brilliant idea.

'Ah,' she said to the man from whom she was buying some fruit, 'I would dearly like some of your fruit, but I have no money.'

The shopkeeper shrugged his shoulders at this, but Nazira went on.

'My husband has fallen on hard times. A more honest, hard-working man you could not find, but there has been a terrible mistake and he has been wrongfully imprisoned by the Caliph.'

As Nazira told this tale a small tear trickled down her cheek. The shopkeeper felt very sorry for her and gave her some fruit saying how sorry he was to hear her story. Nazira, keeping her sad looks, was secretly delighted. Before going home she tried her story, and her acting, on other shopkeepers and collected enough food for a splendid meal.

That night, she and Amin ate well. When they had finished Amin said, 'That was lovely, and it was free, all free!'

So the trickery continued. Amin crept to and from work so early and late that nobody saw him. Nazira got more skilful at this deceitful begging. Then one day she got a shock.

'Now my good woman,' said the man who sold the fruit. 'We've been talking about you down here at the market. The Caliph is a fair man and he can't know you are having to beg like this. Some of us are going to see him and tell him your story.'

Gulping down her shock at this Nazira managed to protest.

'No, no,' she said. 'My husband will be made to suffer more if you do this.'

That night she and Amin discussed this new problem.

'Right,' said Amin. 'We'll just have to try your cousins, and my aunts and uncles now.'

So for the next week or two Nazira told her piteous story to all the relatives she and Amin had. They felt sorry for her and gave her what food they could spare.

'Oh yes, it's still working,' said Amin one night after they had finished their late meal and were counting their ever-growing hoard of treasure. But then, the next day, Nazira found one of her cousins saying the same as the shopkeeper had said. 'We can't let you suffer like this Nazira,' said her cousin, 'we must see the

Caliph.'

Well, Nazira again persuaded them not to, but now neither shopkeepers nor relatives could be begged from. That night the greedy, dishonest couple thought long and hard and Amin finally had an idea.

'The Caliph's got so many jewels,' he said, 'that he'll never notice if I steal one occasionally. Then you can take it to the market, say that it has been given by one of your cousins, and buy food with it. Then we'll still be getting everything for nothing!'

'Brilliant,' said Nazira, and so they began the new scheme.

Now the Caliph, as has already been said, was no fool. He soon realised that jewels were disappearing and so he asked all the merchants and traders in the city to watch out for them—and to tell him who was buying things with them. Within a few days he had got this information from the market. Amin and Nazira were arrested. When their house was searched four heavy bags of money and stolen jewels were discovered.

The Caliph ordered the couple to be brought before him. Amin and Nazira stood, terrified, waiting for what they were sure would be a death sentence.

'No,' said the Caliph. 'I will not sentence you to death. Instead your bags of treasure will be tied round your necks and you will be sent out into the city. Nobody will be allowed to give or sell you anything.'

At first Amin and Nazira were relieved but after a few days they felt very differently. They were exhausted, starving, friendless and in pain from the heavy bags. The Caliph sent for them again.

'Well?' he said.

'Sire forgive us,' they said. 'Please let us use our money to pay back our debts to you, the shopkeepers and our cousins. All we want is to work honestly for an honest wage again.'

The Caliph ordered this to be done. Amin and Nazira were cured of their greed and became one of the most honest and hard-working couples in the Kingdom.

adapted from *Folk Tales of Iran* by A. Dhar

12.   An Unusual Roman

Capernaum lay under the blazing sun on the shores of the Sea of Galilee. Fishing boats could be seen almost everywhere and the barracks of the Roman garrison stood importantly in the town.

In a house near these barracks lived a Roman Centurion. He was a very important man who not only commanded a hundred soldiers, but also had many slaves to do exactly as he told them. Many such powerful Romans of the time were cruel men who thought that keeping people in constant fear was the best way of controlling them.

The centurion at Capernaum, however, was an exception. He treated his troops and his slaves well, knew their names and cared about their well being. So, when one of his hardest working slaves became very ill, he was most concerned about it. Again, unlike many Romans he had several Jewish friends and he asked their advice.

'Well,' said one of these friends, 'this man Jesus has done some marvellous healing but . . .'

'Will you ask him if he can heal this poor fellow?' said the centurion. 'Don't ask him to come to my house because I know how difficult that might be for him.'

So the Jewish friends of the centurion went to seek Jesus and they told him the whole story. Jesus listened and then he said to them, 'There are many Jews who do not have the trust and kindness of this Roman officer. He must be a man to admire.'

The slave made a complete recovery from his illness.

13.   The Leper

The Punjab is a flat district in northern India which is near to the foothills of the Himalayan mountains. The people who live here often call the area the 'land of five rivers' and it was here that many stories of Nanak, the great teacher of Sikhs, were first heard.

In one small village in this land, Guru (teacher) Nanak arrived. It was almost dark and Nanak had been travelling all day. He was desperately in need of somewhere to sleep.

'Can you help me friend?' he said to a passing villager. 'Is there anyone in this village who will allow me to stay in their house for the night?'

The villager looked at the stranger and a sly expression crossed his face.

'Try that house over there,' he said, pointing towards a building which appeared to be a very poorly cared for hut.

'Thank you,' replied Nanak and went over to knock on the door which had been pointed out to him.

On hearing the sound the owner came to the doorway. At once Nanak saw that he was dreadfully scarred with the disease of leprosy. Nanak spoke calmly to him.

'I am tired and I need somewhere to spend the night. May I stay in your house?'

The leper's warm face eased into a sad smile.

'You would be more than welcome to my friend—but you see my situation. Everyone in this village drives me away from them. I'm never spoken to and I'm treated cruelly. It was somebody's idea of a joke that you should be sent to this house.'

'What you have suffered does not seem to have made you less kind. Come, I think we have much to talk about,' replied Nanak.

The next morning when Nanak went on his way the people of the village were amazed to see that the leper had been healed.

14. The Box

The dying old man clasped his friend's hand.

'Friend, please look after my wife and son and take care of my cattle until the boy is old enough to do so himself.'

'Of course I will,' said the old man's friend, whose name was Rahara. But, afterwards he took all the cattle for himself and kept the boy and his mother living in poverty.

The old man however had given his wife a piece of paper saying that the boy should have all the cattle when he became a man. The years passed and Marouba, that was the son's name, became a man. When his mother gave him the paper, he read it and went to Rahara to claim what was his.

'You tell me this tale,' said Rahara, 'but where is your proof?'

'Here, on this piece of paper,' replied Marouba.

'Show me,' said the treacherous Rahara, and when the young man gave him the paper he put it in his mouth and swallowed.

'Now where is the proof?' he said unpleasantly.

Marouba went to the chief of the village with his story. The chief listened carefully and then sent for Rahara. Rahara of course said that Marouba was telling lies.

'I will decide who is telling the truth tomorrow,' said the chief. 'Be at the market place at sunrise.'

The next morning Marouba and his mother and Rahara and his wife went to the market place.

The chief was waiting for them and in front of him a long, heavy looking box stood on the ground.

'Whichever two of you can carry this box round the village in the shortest time will help me decide who is telling the truth,' said the chief. 'Start now.'

Marouba didn't see how this would help the chief to decide who was telling the truth, but he picked up one end of the box. His mother took hold of the other end and they staggered off. They had not gone very far when Marouba's mother, who was old, had to stop for a rest.

'The box is so heavy,' she said. 'Rahara and his wife will be sure to carry it quicker than we can.'

'Well,' said Marouba, 'we at least know we are telling the truth. We can only hope that justice is done.'

Eventually they got back to the square and Rahara and his wife took over the carrying.

'Come on,' said Rahara, 'we can go faster than they did. Then when we get back that old fool, the chief, will think we are telling the truth. Marouba will never get his cattle then.'

Sure enough Rahara and his wife took the shortest time. Smiling with triumph the cunning thief put down the box. As he did so he was amazed when the lid opened—and two men climbed out.

'So,' said the chief, 'thank you for carrying my two wise men round the village. I am sure they have some interesting things to tell me.'

Of course, when the wise men told the chief what they had heard, his decision was easy. Marouba was given not only his cattle, but Rahara's as well. Then Rahara was sent away from the village in disgrace.

adapted from *Stories Told round the World* by T. Zinkin

15.   Reminders

The king looked at the long line of prisoners marching past him and smiled in triumph.

'Another great victory,' he thought to himself. 'I'll go and congratulate my men now.'

So he moved over to the part of the battlefield where his own troops were resting after their victory. Suddenly, as he looked closely at them, they didn't seem very much different from the men he had defeated. Exhausted men slept where they had sat down, the wounded lay groaning in pain, even those who were standing around looked drained and weary.

For the first time in his life the king was shocked at what he saw.

'For years I've been winning battles,' he thought to himself. 'More and more of India has become mine—but at what cost?'

He thought again of the exhausted faces, the ruined bodies, the women widowed, the families made homeless.

For some days after this latest battle the king worried about what he ought to do. Then he sought the advice of some monks who told him of the Buddha's ideas about peace and contentment.

At once the king began to turn his new thoughts into actions. Instead of planning the capture of more territory he set about making that which he had more pleasant to live on. Beautiful gardens, better homes, more care for the people soon began to make his kingdom a much happier place to live in.

'If I've had the wrong ideas for so many years,' thought the king, 'how many other people have as well? I'd better put some reminders round my kingdom so that everybody can see them.'

Immediately he ordered his stonemasons to get to work. They carved pillars of stone which were then placed all over the kingdom. Each pillar carried a message on it: 'Care for Others; Honesty; Avoid Selfishness' and so on. The pillars became reminders of a king who changed his mind and they have stood, displaying their messages, for hundreds of years.

16. Advice from the Katha Upanishad

Think of the body as a chariot.
Think of thoughts as the driver.
Think of the senses as the horses.

He who has no understanding,
Whose mind is not held firm,
Whose senses are uncontrolled,
Is like a vicious horse out of the control of its driver.

He who has understanding,
Whose mind is held firm,
Whose senses are under control,
Is like a good horse in the hands of a firm driver.

adapted from the original

17. Who Is to Blame?

The wise king looked at the creatures lined up in front of him.

'Well,' he said. 'I understand you have a problem, Otter. Let's hear about it.'

'Your Majesty,' replied the otter. 'I went to fish in the river and I left my children to be looked after by Deer. When I came back they had all been trampled on. Now I want justice.'

'What have you got to say about this Deer?' asked the king.

'It is true my Lord,' said the Deer. 'I did trample on the otter's children and I am very, very sorry. Unfortunately I couldn't help it.'

'What do you mean?'

'Well—there I was looking after them when the woodpecker sounded the war alarm. Immediately I had to do the war dance, and I trampled on the young.'

'Why did you sound the war alarm?' asked the king pointing to the woodpecker.

'Duty, your Majesty,' replied the woodpecker. 'I must sound the war alarm when I see Lizard wearing his sword—and I did.'

'This case gets stranger,' murmered the king. 'Why were you wearing your weapon Lizard?'

'Because I saw the tortoise wearing his armour your Majesty,' replied the lizard.

'And what have you got to say Tortoise?' went on the king.

'It's quite true my Lord,' answered the tortoise. 'I put on my armour because I saw the crab carrying his axe.'

'Is this true, Crab?'

'Yes your Majesty, but I only armed myself because I saw the crayfish with his spear.'

Crayfish was the last of the creatures in the line and so far he had said nothing.

'Now, Crayfish,' said the king. 'This has all finally finished with you. Why were you waving your spear?'

'I had to your Majesty. I saw the otter swimming down the river to attack and hunt my children.'

The king stroked his chin and turned to look at the otter.

'So now we know why your children were trampled—and who was really to blame for the whole thing.'

18. How We Are Judged

The court gathered together was a strange one. Standing beside the weighing scales was a creature with the body of a man and the head of a dog. His name was Anubis. Beside Anubis was a creature with the body of a man and the head of a bird. This was Thoth, who wrote down the results of the court's judgement.

'Is she ready?' Anubis asked Thoth.

'Yes,' replied Thoth, 'she is being brought in now.'

A woman wearing a white robe was led slowly into the court room.

'Now woman,' said Anubis. 'You have died and you have come here to be judged. You know the rules?'

The woman nodded and the dog-headed god moved nearer to the scales. In one of the pans he placed the woman's heart and held it there until he was ready to place the lightest looking feather onto the other balance.

When both objects were in place he gently let go of the scales. For a moment there was a slight movement and then everything stayed still.

'Congratulations,' said Anubis, 'the scales show that your heart and the Feather of Truth balance perfectly. This shows that you have lived a life full of kindness and consideration. You may now pass through to the peace and beauty of the Fields of Yaru.'

19. The Man Who Lived for Ever

Gilgamesh had heard stories about a man who lived for ever—and he was determined to find him. After a long, hard journey he had finally arrived at the sea at the end of the world.

'Boatman,' Gilgamesh called to the ferryman who stood beside his old and leaking boat. 'I want to find Utnapishtim, the man who lives for ever.'

After much persuasion the ferryman agreed to take Gilgamesh to the island where Utnapishtim lived. For days the two men rowed over a sea that was still, empty and without life. Eventually they reached a bleak, bare island. The boatman put his passenger ashore and then rowed a little way out to wait for him.

Gilgamesh did not have to look for Utnapishtim because he was there, sitting on the shore, looking incredibly old. His skin was like old parchment, a few wisps of white hair covered his head and he was bent and bowed as if carrying the cares of the world.

'I have come,' said Gilgamesh, 'to find the secret of being able to live for ever. To find this secret I have made a great journey here to the end of the world.'

'Every man must die,' whispered Utnapishtim in a voice like the rustle of dead leaves.

'Every man—but you,' replied Gilgamesh.

'Very well,' said the old, bent figure. 'Listen carefully.'

Then, staring out of pale, tired eyes he told his story.

'Thousand of years ago the gods made men. After a time they saw how men quarrelled and killed each other and made trouble. They decided then that the world would be a better place without men so they prepared a great flood to drown all.

'Now it so happened that the water-god, Ea, wanted some men and animals to survive. So he told me about the flood that was coming and warned me to build a boat to save my family and animals. I was not allowed to warn anybody else.

'The flood came and it was terrifying. By the time six days had passed everything and everyone had been drowned; only those in my boat survived. Finally, I sent out birds to see if they could find food. First a dove went and then returned. Next a swallow went and then returned. The next bird I sent was a raven. When it did not return I knew it had found food and shelter and that the flood was going down. Soon we landed and were safe.'

'What happened then?' asked Gilgamesh.

'The great god Ea came to see me.'

'And?'

'Because I had done exactly what he had ordered he gave me a gift.'

'What was it.'

'It was the gift of eternal life.'

'How marvellous!'

'I do not think so,' went on Utnapishtim. 'Look around you. What do you see? Emptiness, loneliness, nothing—and all because I had to live on this desolate island so that none could find out about this terrible gift I was given.'

Gilgamesh looked round. As he did so he thought of the things which made life worth living—friendship, beauty, enjoying shared pleasures. Man was not made to live forever he thought.

adapted from *The Epic of Gilgamesh* by N.K. Sanders

20. Money Well Spent

When the famous Sikh guru (teacher) Nanak was a boy his generosity used to irritate his father. Whenever Nanak saw somebody in need he gave what he could to help them. In this way he gave away not only money but food and clothes as well.

Finally Nanak's father decided to teach his son a lesson.

'Now listen to me,' said the father, 'to appreciate the value of money you have got to make some. I am going to give you 20 rupees. Take this money to the market in the city. When you get there use the money to buy things which you can later sell at a profit. When you have increased the 20 rupees come home and tell me how you did it.'

So saying Nanak's father gave him the 20 rupees and sent him on his way. On the way to the city Nanak was joined by two friends. As they passed through villages the three stopped to talk to people and encourage them to lead helpful lives by giving to their neighbours whatever they had to spare.

Eventually Nanak and his friends reached a clearing in the jungle. In this clearing sat a group of holy men. They spent their time praying and relied on people to give them sufficient food to keep them alive. Because of this they were all very thin and weak.

Nanak and his friends spent some time with the holy men, listening to their prayers and discussing the advice they could give to other people. After a day or two Nanak spoke to the other two.

'I think our journey ends here, friends. What better use could this money be put to than buying food to keep up the strength of these wise men.'

So for as long as it lasted Nanak spent the 20 rupees in this way. When it was all gone he went home.

Nanak's father saw him approaching and he was very curious.

'He's been away quite some time,' he thought, 'I wonder how much profit he has made?'

'No profit, father,' replied Nanak, when the question was put to him, 'but the money was well spent.'

He then explained to his father what had happened.

21.   Think before You Judge

'You've got to hand it to him—he knows how to plough a field.'

'He certainly does. I never knew a vicar who could do that before.'

The people in the little village in the middle of England were very impressed with their new vicar. Round about the year 1600 what a man could grow in the fields decided whether he would go hungry or not. Here was a vicar who could not only preach a good sermon, but could plough like a real farmer.

So Richard Greenham, the vicar, was soon very popular. The villagers admired the fact that he could sow and plough as well as they could. They also enjoyed the open air services and prayers which he held out in the fields. Then something happened which began to change their opinion of him.

There came a year when the harvest was very poor and the vicar set about buying as much corn as he could from everybody else in the village.

'Bit funny that,' they said to each other. 'Still we've got to get money from somewhere to buy food for our families.'

So they took the vicar's price but still puzzled. Then one day a rumour went round the village.

'Have you heard, the vicar's bought old Applecroft's barn?'

'No—is that right?'

'Now we know why he was buying up the corn. He's going to store it all for himself.''

'Yes, and when the winter comes, we'll all be hungry but the vicar'll have it all to himself.'

So Richard Greenham's popularity disappeared. He didn't deny that he was buying the barn and he made no effort to explain his activities. People now avoided his eye in the street and crossed over when they saw him coming.

Summer faded into autumn and then a cold and bitter winter descended on the village. When it was at its coldest, Richard Greenham looked at the small congregation in his church one Sunday.

'Now,' he said to them, 'I want to speak to you about the barn full of corn.'

At once they all sat up, paying close attention. Here would be something to tell those who weren't at church!

What the vicar said to them was very simple. Anyone who needed corn could come along to his house and buy it at the cheapest possible price. Anybody who was too poor to buy any would be given some.

As the people in church listened they grew more and more ashamed. Not only had their vicar not been storing the corn for himself but he had even thought long ago what a difficult winter it would be after a poor harvest. All the time Richard Greenham had simply been thinking of others.

22.   A True Friend

Tein-Chi was poor but he was contented. He could grow just enough in his small field to live on. One day Tein-Chi was about to eat a meal in an inn when a huge man came into the building. He sat down next to Tein-Chi.

'You look tired and hungry,' said Tein-Chi, 'would you like to share this fried pork with me?'

'Thank you, my friend,' said the giant, eating Tein-Chi's food hungrily. Soon it was finished and whatever Tein-Chi bought in the way of food and drink the giant ate as if he was starving.

Soon Tein-Chi had no money left so he asked the huge man to go home with him. This the giant did and the two became great friends. Now Tein-Chi was both kind and polite. He kept feeding his new friend's enormous appetite but he was too polite to say that his stocks of food were going down—and he had no money to buy more.

What was worse was the fact that Tein-Chi's neighbours were by no means as kind and honest as he was. As they all lived in a place where there was not much water for their crops they altered the ditches so that when a little rain fell it ran towards their fields—and away from Tein-Chi's.

'It's a pity they are so dishonest,' said Tein-Chi to his friend the huge man. 'If only people weren't so greedy. There is just enough water for all but now my crops won't grow because my neighbours want it all for themselves.'

That night Tein-Chi thought of what he had said to the giant just before he fell asleep. Then, as soon as his eyes closed, he felt very strange. Slowly, opening one eye, he saw that he was no longer in his own bed but floating high above his house on a cloud!

'I must be dreaming,' he thought, 'but . . . who are these people?'

A chariot, pulled by dragons, was coming towards him. Alongside it were men pouring water into clouds.

'Hey, you!' shouted one of the men. 'What are you doing up here?'

'He's my friend, leave him be,' said another voice, and Tein-Chi saw that it was his friend the giant who was carrying a huge wooden pail of water.

'Now Tein-Chi,' said the giant, 'you see me as I really am. We work for the Thunder God spreading rain over the earth. But many long months ago I made a mistake doing this so I was sentenced to live below on earth until I found one really honest man. It took me a long time to find one—and of course the person I found was you, my friend.'

'But . . .' began Tein-Chi.

'No buts,' said the giant. 'Come with me.'

Then he took Tein-Chi directly over his own field and he gave him a huge spoon.

'Now,' said the giant, 'spray your field with water so that your crops will grow well again.'

So, all night long, Tein-Chi worked hard spraying his field. When it was almost morning his friend lowered him to the ground. Next day Tein-Chi saw his crops growing healthily as he worked amongst them.

He never saw the huge stranger again and he might have thought he really had dreamt his journey in the clouds except for the fact that when he had been in the sky he had put a tiny passing star into his pocket. Whenever he thought about how friends should help each other he reached into his pocket—and there was the star to remind him of his great adventure.

23. The Two Chinamen

There were once two Chinamen who we will call Heng and Yong. They were very poor so they decided to leave China and go to Thailand to seek their fortune.

'Now,' said Heng, 'this is what we will do. We will meet again when we have made 500 baths (Thai money). Until we do so neither of us will eat any pork or duck. Do you agree?'

'Oh yes,' said Yong. So they parted.

Heng got a job and worked hard. Whatever spare money he had, he saved. He did not spend any on expensive food like pork or duck. Soon he had enough money to start his own small business. He put his savings into this, worked very hard and began to get rich.

Next Heng got married and built a fine house. At last, after all this he thought to himself:

'I've got far more than 500 baths now and a fine house and business. Now I can start eating pork and duck. I wonder how my old friend Yong is getting on?'

Well the truth was that Yong was not getting on very well. After parting from Heng he too had got a job. However, he didn't keep his promise to himself and he spent much of his money on the expensive food of pork and duck. He wanted to grow rich and not do without anything, both at the same time.

Eventually, although he had nothing like 500 baths, he arrived at the town where Heng lived. He was astonished to see Heng's fine house and felt miserable. Heng was a kind man, however, and so he welcomed his old friend and gave him a house to live in.

Then Heng sent Yong some rice and told him he could take some leaves from a tamarind tree near the house to make the rice taste nicer. As usual Yong was greedy and took, not some leaves, but all of them.

The next day Heng came to see his friend and he saw the bare branches.

'Yong, my friend,' he said, 'you have taken all the leaves so that there will be no more for a long time. If only you had taken a few at a time, others would have been growing for when you needed them. If you seek to have everything now there may be nothing for later.'

Yong listened to his friend's advice. He realised how foolish he had been so he began to work hard and try to think of the future. With Heng's advice he became a rich man too.

adapted from *Folk Tales of Thailand* by P.C.R. Chandhur

24. Quick Thinking

'I'm glad he's here,' thought the stranded motorist, as he watched the R.A.C. patrolman's van come into sight. Minutes later the van pulled into the layby on the busy M23 road near Gatwick.

'Now, Sir, what's the trouble?' asked R.A.C. patrolman, Kevin Brinklow, as he climbed out of his van.

'I wish I knew,' said the motorist, as the two of them moved over to the broken-down car.

'Well, let's have a look,' said Patrolman Brinklow, lifting up the bonnet and looking at the engine.

At that moment there was the terrible sound of tyres squealing on the motorway behind them. This was followed by the even more frightening crunch of two cars hitting each other. Immediately Patrolman Brinklow turned and saw that there had been a serious accident.

Dropping his tool-bag he raced back to his van and quickly backed it across the motorway. As he did so he switched on the beacon and hazard warning lights. Oncoming traffic could now see that there had been an accident and could brake quickly themselves.

Mr. Brinklow then turned towards the wreckage of the two cars. As he did so he could smell the petrol leaking out of their punctured tanks. Ignoring the danger he managed to pull open the driver's door of one of the cars. Reaching inside he carefully eased out the unconscious man and carried him to the safety of the hard shoulder of the road.

By now the smell of petrol was overpowering and as the resourceful patrolman turned back there was a sudden 'whoosh' and the two cars burst into flames.

Racing to his van Mr. Brinklow wrenched out a fire extinguisher and began to use it on the blazing vehicles. Time after time he got as near as he could to the cars only to be driven back by the fierce heat of the flames, By now, however, more help was at hand and the brave patrolman was no longer dealing with things alone.

Later in the year Patrolman Brinklow's courage and quick thinking was rewarded when he received the R.A.C.'s meritorious medal for bravery.

25. A Friend Indeed

'Isn't it marvellous up here!' called out Erwin to his friend as he edged up the mountain side.

'Yes, it's wonderful,' replied Jurgen as he gazed up at the clear blue sky above the snowy mountain peaks.

The 22-year-old young men had just left Munich to spend a week's holiday climbing in the Alps. Now, roped together, they were slowly making their way up a sheer mountain face.

'We should soon be . . .' Erwin started to say, when a piece of equipment that was helping to secure him to the rock face suddenly gave way. Scrambling to hang on with his finger tips he found it impossible and, with a cry, he fell backwards into space.

Horrified Jurgen saw his friend falling past him and then, as the rope between them tightened, he too was plucked like a fly from the mountainside and plunged downwards. For almost 50 metres the two men fell and then crashed, badly injured, onto the rocks below.

'Jurgen . . . Jurgen . . . are you all right?' called out Erwin when he got his breath back.

There was no answer and Erwin, despite his own terrible pain, crawled over to his friend. There, he found that Jurgen had broken both legs and was also suffering from internal injuries and shock.

'I must get help,' thought Erwin, but looking down at his own leg which was broken so badly that he could see the bone, he wondered how he might do this.

Lying back he called and called for help as loudly as he could. Only the wind whistling at the high, lovely Alps answered him.

Soon it was night and, unpacking their rucksacks, Erwin made his friend as comfortable as he possibly could. Then he pulled a blanket over himself and settled down for the long and freezing cold night.

When dawn came, Erwin could see that Jurgen was much weaker. He would obviously not be able to live through another night out there.

'I must get help!' thought Erwin for the hundredth time. Dragging himself painfully towards a nearby bush he cut off some of the thickest branches with his sharp hunting knife. He then tied two of them to his broken leg to act as splints, and from two more he made a crude pair of crutches. Then, almost unable to bear the pain, he set off to seek help.

Six hours later Erwin saw a mountain hut ahead of him. He had struggled for eight hours and was almost frantic with pain and exhaustion. Dragging himself to the door of the hut he knocked loudly—and then, unable to stand the pain any longer, he fainted.

When Erwin recovered consciousness he got a terrific shock. He was lying on an operating table in a hospital and a smiling doctor was bending over him.

'You'll soon be all right now,' said Doctor Burgsteiner. 'We're going to give you something to make you go to sleep again and when you wake up this time your leg will be on the way to mending.'

'No . . .!' Erwin cried, struggling to sit up. 'You must get to my friend.' Then he told the surprised doctor about Jurgen.

Thanks to Erwin the story had a happy ending. When he had fainted at the door of the hut, the mountain guide who was inside had radioed for a helicopter. This had taken Erwin to hospital where he had told the doctor the rest of the story just before his operation.

The same helicopter had then flown back into the mountains—and discovered Jurgen just ten minutes before darkness fell. Later, when both young men were recovering Doctor Burgsteiner told them that Jurgen would certainly have died if he had had to spend another night on the mountains.

26. Remember a Kind Deed

The Emperor was very sick with a raging fever. During the day he did not feel too bad but as soon as darkness fell and he tried to get some sleep he kept getting the most dreadful dreams. Each morning he awoke feeling ever more exhausted.

The Emperor was well liked by his people and many of them wondered what they could do to help. One day two of the Emperor's bravest warriors asked if they could see him.

'Well my friends, what is it you want?' said the Emperor when the two appeared before him.

Bowing low, Wang, one of the warriors said, 'Sir, we have heard about your dreams and we have come to try and help.'

'But first,' went on Shiang, the other warrior, 'we must know what you dream about.'

'Ah,' said the Emperor, 'I dream of demons and evil spirits. Every night they are trying to get in through the door of my palace.'

'Then sir,' said Wang, 'every night when our duties are over we will come and stand as sentries at your door.'

That night the two warriors brought their weapons and, standing on either side of the door to the palace, they stayed there on guard until morning. Night after night they did this and before he went to sleep the Emperor came down to see them. Seeing his two brave and unselfish warriors every night made the Emperor feel much better. Soon he began to sleep soundly, his dreams stopped and he recovered completely from his fever. Then he sent for the two warriors.

'My friends,' he said to them, 'thanks to you I am better. But on each of my door posts I going to put something to remind everybody of your faithfulness.'

So the Emperor ordered a picture to be painted on each door post. These pictures showed two heavily armed warriors on guard. When other people saw them they thought not only of the faithful warriors, but also of the good they had done. And so for many years Chinese people put pictures of warriors on their own door posts to keep away evil spirits.

adapted from *Dragons, Gods and Spirits from Chinese Mythology* by T.T.L. Saunders

27. The Shy Hero

Leonard Skutnik was going home after an ordinary day's work at his office in Washington, U.S.A.

'I'll be glad to get home,' thought Leonard, 'it's so cold.' Pulling his thick overcoat more tightly round him he shuddered as the icy snow swirled downwards.

It was then that he heard the aeroplane. He knew by its noise that it was very low—and then he saw it.

The Air Florida Boeing, Flight 90, had just taken off from Washington's international airport. In such terrible conditions there was ice on the wings and this made it difficult for the plane to gain height quickly.

With engines screaming the Boeing lumbered off the end of the runway and the pilot fought with the controls to gain sufficient height to pass over the bridge which was straight ahead. Despite his efforts it was no use. The plane would not lift and to the horror of Leonard and all the other people watching, it crashed into the bridge and then plunged into the River Potomac.

Within minutes people were racing to the river bank. As they did so a pitifully few heads began to surface above the freezing surface of the river. These were the fortunate passengers who had managed to get out of the sinking plane.

When Leonard reached the river bank he saw a woman struggling desperately to reach the shore. It was obvious that in the intense cold she was not going to make it.

Hurling off his coat, Leonard plunged into the icy water. Within a few seconds he had reached the woman and, taking her in his arms, he swam back to the bank with her. Eager hands helped them both ashore and within minutes she was on her way to hospital.

Leonard shrugged aside the congratulations and, seeing that there was nothing more he could do, set about getting home. Hundreds of people had seen Leonard's bravery, however, and the newspapers and television all told his story the next day. But for his courage, Priscilla Tirado would have died and the tragic accident would have claimed one more victim.

28.　The Voice of Experience

There was once a wise old man who sat beneath a shady tree in the village before sunset every evening. People from far and wide came to ask his advice about all sorts of things.

One day a woman came to see the wise man.

'I need your help, wise one.' she said.

'What is it?' he asked.

'My son eats too many sweet things—he likes sugar in his drinks, he likes to eat sweets and cake. I cannot afford this and I want you to speak to him.'

'What do you want me to say to him?' asked the wise man.

'I want you to forbid him to eat and drink so many sweet things.'

'Bring him to see me at the next full moon,' said the wise man.

The days passed and the woman came back with her son.

'Ah,' said the wise old man. 'I cannot tell your son to stop eating so many sweet things yet. Bring him back at the next full moon.'

The woman was very surprised at this comment. However, she and her son went home, and duly returned at the next full moon. This time the wise old man spoke for some time to the son and told him that he must not eat or drink so many sweet things.

When he had done this the woman stayed behind and spoke to the man of wisdom again.

'Tell me,' she said curiously. 'I cannot understand why it has taken you so long to instruct my son as you have.'

The wise old man smiled.

'Before I could tell your son to give up so many sweet things, I had to see if I could do it myself first.'

adapted from *Folk Tales of Sri Lanka* by M. Ratnatunga

29. Olga, V.C.

During the Second World War two hundred horses were used by men of London's Metropolitan Police Force. These horses and their riders directed fire engines, ambulances, air raid wardens and hundreds of people during London's terrible bombing raids. Three of the horses won the Dickin Medal, the animals' Victoria Cross. This is the story of one of those brave horses.

Police Constable Thwaites was riding Olga through the streets of Tooting in South London in the summer of 1944.

'Steady, steady old girl,' he said as he patted the horse. He had never ridden Olga before and he did not know how she might behave in a crisis. Then, just as he was wondering about this, he heard the dreaded sound of the air raid siren. This meant that some of the Germans' deadly, pilotless flying bombs were approaching the city.

'There, there,' he said to Olga, trying to calm the horse who seemed nervous. No sooner had he spoken than there was a tremendous explosion less than a hundred metres away. Olga stood firm as a row of houses hit by the flying bomb exploded in all directions. Then, a second explosion sent a huge plate glass window crashing down from a nearby shop. It hit the ground with an enormous bang and sent pieces of glass scudding through the air.

With a start of terror Olga turned and bolted from the terrifying scene. Clinging onto the reins P.C. Thwaites tried to control his runaway horse, and within a few minutes he was successful.

'Now,' he murmered to Olga, 'we've got to go back and help.'

Heading the horse back to the area where it had been so frightened, P.C. Thwaites eventually reached the street which had been hit. Olga was quivering with fear but she let herself be led through the noise and smoke and flying dust and brick. Then she stood still as P.C. Thwaites, sitting on her back, directed rescue operations to help the people who had been injured.

Eventually when the fires had been brought under control and the injured taken to hospital, the policeman took his dust-caked and scratched horse back to the stables. For her great devotion to duty Olga was awarded the Dickin Medal.

30.   Gifts

The visitor moved round the temple in Kyoto, Japan, looking at the various objects. Suddenly he saw a rather strange looking rope in what was obviously a place of honour.

'That is rather unusual, isn't it?' he said to the guide who was accompanying him.

'Without that rope this temple would probably not even be here,' replied the guide. 'I'll tell you its story and then you'll see what I mean.'

The guide began his story with an explanation.

'Many years ago no Japanese girl ever cut her hair. As she grew to be a woman it was wound in thick coils round her head. The only exception to this custom was if the husband of a Japanese lady died, then half of her hair was cut off and buried with her husband. So you can see that long hair was very much a custom of the time.

Well, when work began on the temple in Kyoto the builders soon encountered a problem. As the temple was to be very large they could not find a rope either long or strong enough to be used to haul heavy wooden beams up to the necessary height.

The women of Kyoto heard about this problem and they decided that if they wanted the temple to be built they would have to make a sacrifice. So they all got together, cut off each other's hair and wound a rope. It was immensely strong and between two and three hundred metres in length.

With this rope the building of the temple was able to go ahead. Since its completion the rope has always had a place of honour in it, to remind people that nothing worthwhile is ever achieved easily.

31. Modesty

All the great religions of the world suggest that if we do something which helps other people we should be modest about it. This is not always easy, but the action of an off-duty London policeman provides a fine example of such modesty.

It was very much a normal sort of day on the London Underground and trains carrying hundreds of passengers criss-crossed beneath the city. Then a mysterious fire broke out in a tunnel between Goodge Street and Warren Street stations.

Immediately dense smoke choked the tunnel and four trains carrying about 900 people were trapped. Driver John Gutteridge tried to drive one of the trains to safety but was overcome by smoke. There was only one thing to do: somebody had to lead the choking passengers out of the dark and terrifying tunnel.

It was then that one of the passengers took charge. Organising a group of people from the train he was on, he took them back to the safety of the station. Then, ignoring the killing fumes as best he could, he plunged back into the tunnel to bring out the next group. Repeatedly he did this until almost everybody was safe.

By now more help was at hand and as people staggered to safety they were quickly given help. Fifteen were taken immediately to hospital but one man died before he got there. Soon the chaos was overcome. Everybody had been got out of the tunnel, and the fire had been put out.

It was then that many of the survivors looked round to thank the man who had helped to save their lives. He could not be found. Having done all he could to help he had then quietly slipped away on his own business. All that could be found out about him was that he was an off-duty policeman and a regular passenger.

A few days later when the government was investigating how the fire had started, the leader of the inquiry, Major Charles Rose, said, 'We must try to find this officer and thank him for his work. He did a marvellous job.'

32. What the Bear Said

'How much further?' asked John.

'Oh we'll soon be at the village now,' replied Peter. 'Once we are through this forest you will see it.'

'I don't like the look of this forest much. Is it dangerous?'

'Well, there are bears and wolves in it, and if they are hungry we had better watch out.'

No sooner had John said this than the forest path the two men were walking along got very narrow. Suddenly, crashing through the undergrowth in front of them, appeared a bear. With a snarl it stopped in the middle of the path, barring their way.

Two things then happened. Peter with a cry of fear left John, threw himself through the bushes and climbed to safety in a nearby tree. John, left alone to face the now advancing beast remembered an old saying, 'bears will not touch dead men'. Dropping to the ground he lay absolutely motionless.

Shuffling and growling the bear advanced up the path. When it reached John it moved carefully all round him and then lowered its head to his neck and shoulders. For several seconds it sniffed whilst John strove to keep quite still. Finally, deciding that the man really was dead, the bear turned and lumbered off into the forest.

To make quite sure it did not return John continued to lie quite still. Then he was conscious of a movement beside him. It was Peter, back from the tree.

'I saw all that,' said Peter, 'even the bear talking to you. What did he say?'

'Oh—only that a person who runs away at the first sign of trouble is hardly likely to be a reliable friend,' replied John.

adapted from Aesop

33. Bus to the Rescue

The number 2 bus was on its last early morning trip to Stockwell Garage. There were no passengers on board when conductress Mrs. Velma McCrae suddenly got a shock.

Running alongside the bus was a man indicating that he wanted it to stop. This would not have surprised Mrs. McCrae, but the fact that he was wearing nothing but a pair of trousers certainly did!

'He must be mad,' thought the conductress to herself, but then she noticed something else out of the corner of her eye. Smoke was spiralling out of a house in nearby Robson Road. Quickly Mrs. McCrae signalled to driver Sydney Evans to stop. As he did so the man outside clambered aboard.

'Quick, I need help,' he gasped. 'House on fire.'

Acting immediately Mr. Evans turned the bus towards Robson Road and skidded to a stop in front of it. He could now see that thick smoke was billowing from an upstairs window, and there was somebody trapped in the room.

Thinking quickly Mr. Evans reversed his bus towards the front of the house. Meanwhile Mrs. McCrae and Terry Parker, the man they had picked up, scrambled up to the top deck. Once there they opened the rear top deck emergency window.

By now the back of the bus was very close to the windows from which all the smoke was coming. Inside the bedroom Mrs. Joan Parker held out her 6-year-old daughter, Jacqueline. Reaching out from the bus Mrs. McCrae helped the frightened child to safety. Then Mrs. Parker scrambled out of the house into the bus.

By now the fire brigade had been called and an engine was approaching. Leaving Mrs. Parker and her child with the firemen, the number 2 bus continued on its journey.

Later, London Transport congratulated Mr. Evans and Mrs. McCrae on their quick thinking which had helped to save two lives.

34.   When in Danger . . .

It was a day of intense heat. The sky was a cloudless blue, heat shimmered above the baked ground and trees were motionless. The river flowed slowly along its bed but the water looked cool and inviting.

A lion strode out of the bushes and bent to drink. Just as he was about to put his mouth in the water another lion appeared at his side.

'Just you wait a minute,' said the first lion. 'I was here first so I drink first.'

'That's foolishness,' said the second lion. 'There's plenty of water here for both of us.'

'You don't know that,' said the first lion. 'In any case, you must wait your turn.'

'I don't see why I should.'

So the two beasts stood in the sweltering sun and argued with each other. Both were hot and desperately thirsty but neither would give way in the argument.

Suddenly, whilst he was talking, the first lion noticed some shadows flicker across the sun. He stopped what he was saying, looked up, and then spoke again.

'Ha—look up there.'

'Yes,' replied the second lion. 'Vultures.'

'How foolish we are,' went on the first lion. 'Those creatures know we are arguing down here. They are waiting for us to fight so that they can come down and feed on the body of the loser.'

'You're right,' said the second lion. 'Drink first, my friend. I am sorry to have been so difficult.'

'I was just as much to blame,' replied the first lion.

And so they drank from the river together and the vultures flew off in search of prey elsewhere.

35. The Good Life

There was once a young priest who wanted to live to serve people as best he could. In order to prepare himself for this he went to see a much older priest who was loved and respected by everybody.

'Have you any advice you could give me?' asked the young priest.

'Certainly,' replied the older man. 'Go and stay at the village inn for a week and take notice of the innkeeper.'

The young priest did this. The days went by and he did not see the innkeeper doing anything special or outstanding or holy. Puzzled at the old priest's advice the younger man spoke to the innkeeper.

'What do you think is important about what you do all day?'

'Why,' said the innkeeper. 'It is all important. I must see that all drinks are given fairly, that the food is well prepared, that the bedrooms are clean. I must make sure that everybody gets value for money, enjoys their stay and would be glad to come back.'

Having said this the innkeeper hurried back to work.

The week ended and the young priest went back to see his adviser.

'Well,' said the old priest, 'How did you get on?'

The young priest told him, mentioning particularly what the innkeeper had said about the importance of his day.

'Ah,' said the older man, 'now you know the answer to the advice you asked me for.'

36. Three for Supper

'Do you think it looks enough John?'

The poor woman looked at the table with the supper laid out on it. The meal was set for three places but there did not look to be too much food.

'Well Mary,' replied the husband, 'It's all we've got and its not every night that Jesus calls at a poor man's house for supper.'

'You're right there,' replied Mary. 'Oh I do hope . . .'

Before Mary could finish speaking there was a loud knock on the door.

'Do you think . . .'

'I don't know, but I'll go and see.'

John opened the door. Outside stood a thin beggar in ragged clothes.

'I'm sorry to disturb you,' said the beggar, 'but I haven't had a decent meal for days. I wondered if you could spare me a bite?'

John hesitated for only a moment, then he spoke.

'Of course, come in.'

When Mary saw the beggar she took some of the food from the table and put it on a plate. This was handed to the beggar who ate gratefully. Soon he was gone, expressing his thanks as he left.

'Ah well, you and I will just have to eat a little less when Jesus gets here,' said Mary, looking at the thinned out spread of food. No sooner had she spoken than there was another knock at the door. This time Mary went to see who it was and found another beggar standing there.

'Could you spare anything to eat please?' he asked.

Mary looked at him. He was only a boy and his torn and ragged clothes covered a pitifully thin body.

'Fetch the lad in,' said John, who was looking over his wife's shoulder. 'To tell you the truth I've completely lost my appetite—give him what I was going to have for supper.'

When the boy had eaten he left the poor couple, thanking them for their kindness.

'Oh dear, there's not much left,' said Mary. No sooner had she spoken than there was yet another knock on the door. John answered it and found Jesus standing on the step.

'Come in, come in,' said John. 'We were a bit worried about you. We thought perhaps you weren't coming.'

Jesus smiled.

'Oh yes John. I've been here twice already.'

37. Corporal Supanivalu

During the Second World War fighting took place on the Soloman Islands between the Allied forces and the Japanese. Some of the best fighters in the jungle conditions were the soldiers from Fiji.

One day a corporal named Supanivalu was leading a group of ten Fijian soldiers through the jungle in the Soloman Islands when they met a Japanese patrol. Both sides opened fire and Corporal Supanivalu was wounded immediately. The rest of the Fijians took cover and before long they were pinned down by heavy Japanese fire.

Supanivalu was ahead of the rest of his men and he knew that the Japanese re-inforcements were nearby and would soon reach the scene of the action. If his men did not retreat immediately they would be cut off.

'Get back to base at once,' he shouted. There was no movement behind him and he realised the trouble. His troops knew he was wounded and they did not want to leave without him. He also knew that if they waited they would be killed and if they tried to take him with them he would be such a burden that the Japanese would soon catch them up.

Corporal Supanivalu made up his mind. Staggering painfully to his feet he stood in full view of the enemy. He just managed to shout a last order to retreat before a volley of Japanese bullets killed him.

The story of the brave corporal's sacrifice did not end there, however. His soldiers got back to base and told of their leader's great courage. As a result of this Corporal Supanivalu was awarded a posthumous medal. It was the Victoria Cross, one of the world's greatest medals for bravery, and he was the only Fijian ever to win it.

The story still does not end there. In order to remind everybody of this man's courage, and the concern of his comrades who would not leave and save their own lives, the Fijian government founded a scholarship. This is awarded for study every year and the Supanivalu Scholarship continues to this day.

38. The Gift You Deserve

Audun lived in Iceland many years ago. He looked after his mother well, he was a very honest man and a good worker. The person who he admired more than anyone else was King Svein, the King of Denmark. Audun thought King Svein was the fairest and kindest king in the world.

At about this this time Audun's master said he could have a long holiday from his work on the farm. Audun had a brilliant idea.

'I'll make a journey to Denmark,' he thought. 'I'll take all the money I've saved up, call in at Greenland and buy a polar bear. Then I'll go on to Denmark and give the polar bear to King Svein as a present.'

Now polar bears were considered presents fit for kings at this time and any king would be very pleased to receive one.

Audun's journey began. First of all his ship went to Greenland and he spent all his money buying a magnificent polar bear. Then the ship made its next stop at Norway.

'Look at that creature!' shouted one of the Norwegians.

'Isn't it beautiful?'

'It must be worth a fortune.'

Everybody crowded round to admire the bear because such animals were hardly ever seen in Norway. Then King Harald heard about it. He sent for Audun.

'Now my man,' said the King of Norway. 'What present can I give you in exchange for that polar bear?'

'None, your Majesty,' said the Icelander.

The King offered large sums of money next but Audun refused to accept. Then he told Harald that he was taking the bear as a gift for King Svein because he admired the Danish King more than anybody else in the world.

'What?' said King Harald.

Now Harald hated Svein and he was amazed that Audun dared to say this to him. After some thought, however, he decided that Audun must be very brave to do so.

'Very well,' said Harald, 'promise me only this—come back and tell me what Svein gives you in return for the bear.'

So Audun eventually arrived in Denmark. By now he had no money left to feed either himself or the bear. He went to the Danish King's palace and the first person he saw there was Aki, the King's steward. He told Aki his story.

Aki was a crafty man.

'Oh yes I'll give you both food,' he said, 'but in return you must say the bear is a present from you *and* me.'

To save his bear from starvation Audun had to agree. Some days later he saw the King.

'Your Majesty,' he said. 'I have brought a polar bear to Denmark. I wanted to give him to you as a present, but now I only own half of him.'

The King asked Audun to explain. When he heard the whole story he was furious with Aki, who was banished. Then he said to Audun:

'This is a wonderful present. You must be rewarded.'

Well, as a reward Audun was sent to Rome to meet other Christians and then when he got back the King of Denmark gave him more presents. These were a ship, all its cargo, a purse full of silver and a silver arm band.

'Now', said King Svein, 'Good luck. I hope you will keep that silver arm band for ever. It should only be given away if you meet a really great man who deserves it.'

Audun then set off in his new ship to go home to Iceland. He had remembered his promise to King Harald, however, so he called at Norway.

'You're back,' said Harald. 'Well, what did Svein give you?'

Audun told him. When he had finished Harald spoke again.

'I would have given you everything except the silver purse and arm band. I think the ship and cargo would have been fair.'

'There is one more thing your Majesty,' said Audun.

'Oh?' replied Harald.

Audun took the silver band from his arm and bent on one knee.

'I would like you to accept this gift, Sire,' he said. 'You could have taken the bear from me for nothing—and yet you allowed me to take it and give it to your greatest enemy. King Svein said I should only give this to a great man who deserves it. Please accept it.'

King Harald was pleased to take the gift and he admired Audun's thoughtfulness. In return he gave the Icelander some presents to take home with him. So, with his adventures over, Audun returned to his mother and lived happily for many more years.

39. Miracles

Why, who makes much of a miracle?
As to me I know of nothing else but miracles,
Whether I walk the streets of Manhattan,
Or dart my sight over the roofs of houses toward the sky,
Or wade with naked feet along the beach just in the edge of the water,
Or stand under trees in the woods,
Or watch honey-bees around the hive on a summer forenoon,
Or animals feeding in the fields,
Or birds, or the wonderfulness of insects in the air,
Or the wonderfulness of the sundown, or of the stars shining so quiet and
    bright,
Or the exquisite delicate thin curve of the new moon in spring;
These with the rest, one and all, are to me miracles,
The whole referring, yet each distinct and in its place.

To me every hour of the light and dark is a miracle,
Every cubic inch of space is a miracle,
Every square yard of the surface of the earth is spread with the same,
Every foot of the interior swarms with the same.

To me the sea is a continual miracle,
The fishes that swim—the rocks—the motion of the waves—ships with men
    in them,
What stranger miracles are there?

an extract from 'Miracles' by Walt Whitman

40.   Spiders' Webs

There was a tingle in the air, Morag thought. A kind of excitement, an expecting. It was a something's-going-to-happen day. She gazed all about her, seeing miles and miles or moorland and mountains, feeling herself alone in the middle of them. It was all very wonderful, very beautiful and Morag felt very happy.

Now she was passing the blackthorn hedge. In springtime, it was a foam of white blossom, but now it was bare and leafless. No, not bare, for it was covered with spiders' webs. So many of them there were.

She stopped to peer into a tunnel-like web and thought she could see the spider, right at the very back. But it was hard to be sure. In front of the tunnel there stretched a long gossamer thread, looped from thorn to thorn. Morag touched it very gently.

Drops of frosted dew, like little glass beads, hung from the thread. They weighed it down in a sweeping curve, a necklace of silver drops threaded on gossamer. But when she tried most carefully to take her finger away, the thread clung to it and she could not shake it off.

It seemed to Morag very important that she should not break the thread.

'I shall count to five,' she decided. 'If it won't be letting me go by that time, then I shall have to walk on, even if I do break it.'

Ever since she could remember, Morag had counted things in fives. If there were five of anything, then everything was all right. She could not have said why this was so, it just was.

She counted to five as she tried to move her finger without breaking the thread. In spite of all her care, the thread broke.

from *The Black Gull of Corrie Lachan* by M. MacAlpine

41. A Miraculous Escape

Making bricks from clay in the hot Egyptian sun was a hard enough task without the cruel treatment which the Hebrews received from their harsh taskmasters.

So, when Rameses, the Pharoah, eventually agreed to let the Hebrews leave their slavery in Egypt, Moses urged his people to make their escape without delay. There was not even time to bake proper bread with yeast in it so the supplies the Hebrews took with them consisted of flat pieces of 'unrisen' bread.

Then the great journey began. Suspecting that the Pharoah would change his mind and order the Hebrews back, Moses led his people as quickly as possible towards a swampy area known as the Sea of Reeds. They had just reached the fringe of this 'sea' when shouted warnings from the rear confirmed Moses's fears. The Egyptian army was in pursuit.

Faced with what appeared an impossible situation, Moses ordered the people to continue going forward. As they did so two things happened: darkness fell and a sudden strong east wind held at bay the shallow waters which usually flooded over this area.

In the morning the Pharoah could hardly believe that the Hebrews had been able to get across this treacherous land so easily. Thinking that what they could do, he could also, he ordered his troops to advance. At dawn, however, the wind had dropped and the water began to advance over the marsh. Where the soft ground had just held sufficiently for people to walk over it, there was now thick cloying mud which held horses and chariots in an ever increasing grip. The Hebrews had escaped.

Today Jewish people remember this great escape at the Festival of the Passover.

42. A Cat

She had a name among the children;
But no one loved though someone owned
Her, locked her out of doors at bedtime
And had her kittens duly drowned.

In Spring, nevertheless, this cat
Ate blackbirds, thrushes, nightingales,
And birds of bright voice and plume of flight,
As well as scraps from neighbours' pails.

I loathed and hated her for this;
One speckle on a thrush's breast
Was worth a million such; and yet
She lived long, till God gave her rest.

Edward Thomas

43.   The First Human Being

The god Pund-jel looked at the tree and rubbed the side of his nose with his finger.

'Why not?' he thought. 'I could make them now, and that tree gives me just the idea of how I might do it.'

Taking his huge, sharp knife he slashed three pieces of bark from the tree. He then spread the pieces of bark on the ground and scooped up some clay from the ground nearby. Working the clay in his hands until it was soft and pliable, he then spread it out on one piece of the bark.

Then he picked up another of the bark pieces, took some of the clay and began to shape it against the wood. First he smoothed out two feet-like shapes, then legs, a body and arms. Finally and very carefully he covered the end of the bark with the shape of a head.

'That looks good,' he thought to himself. 'Now to make the other one.'

Picking up his materials again he made another human figure and then laid it down beside the first one.

'They are not quite right,' he thought, when he had finished both. 'But I know what they need.'

Taking up his knife again he went back to the tree and cut from it some long, thin strands of bark. Then, taking this to his wood and clay carvings, he arranged it carefully on each of their heads. Now the figures had 'hair'.

Next Pund-jel laid aside his tools, got to his feet and danced in a circle round the two clay and wood figures. When he stopped he bent over each. First he blew air into each of their noses, then into each of their mouths, then into each of their navels. Then, he danced round them again. When he had finished his dance this time he commanded both of the figures to get up, to move and to speak.

So the first human beings were created.

44. How Man Got Fire

The coyote crouched on all fours looking at the strange scene on top of the mountain. From behind the bush where he hid he could see the fire blazing. Every so often one of the three creatures who guarded it would throw on more wood to keep the blaze going.

Coyote was there because down below the mountain man had no fire. In the summer he was warm and happy but in the long winters he grew cold, frightened and hungry. Only Coyote knew that fire was secretly kept at the top of this mountain. The three creatures who guarded it did not care about man. They wanted it only for themselves and would never share its secrets.

For days Coyote watched the guardians of the fire. One of them was always near it and they took turns to sleep and eat. But there was one time when it was less well guarded than others. Just before dawn each morning the guardian on duty went to wake one of the others to take over. Usually he took a few minutes to get up and reach his post. Coyote decided that this would be the time when he would strike.

The next morning when the darkness began to change to the first grey of dawn Coyote was ready. As the fire guardians prepared their change-over he slid down from his hiding place, siezed a piece of fire and turned to race down the mountainside.

The guardians of the fire saw him as he turned. With screeches of fury they raced in pursuit. As fast as he could move Coyote knew that he could never out-run creatures like these with special powers.

However, he had made a plan. As he raced down the mountain he kept throwing the fire to other animals who were waiting for him at various places. This confused the fire guardians who had to twist and turn not knowing who they had to chase next.

Nevertheless they were gaining once more when the last of the animals threw the fire into wood. Immediately wood took the fire into its own body and it disappeared. The fire guardians were furious but they could not get the missing piece of fire back. They returned to the mountain.

Now Coyote knew that he had succeeded. He next showed man how to get the fire back by rubbing two pieces of wood together. Soon man knew more and more about fire and it helped him through the long, dark winters.

45. Silent, But ...

I may be silent, but
I'm thinking.
I may not talk, but
Don't mistake me for a wall.

Tsuboi Shigeji
(translated by G. Bownas
and A. Thwaite)

46. How Mohammed Was Saved

Mohammed and Abu Bakr were trying to escape from the soldiers who were after them. The desert was hot and the two men were tired. Then they saw a cave ahead of them.

'Look,' said Abu Bakr, 'there's a cave, we could hide in there.'

Mohammed smiled but did not say anything and the two of them entered the cave. They went as far into it as they could and sat down. Then Abu Bakr began to look worried.

'If we found this cave so easily,' he said, 'then so will the soldiers. We'll be trapped because there is no other way of getting out.'

'Listen, my friend,' said Mohammed, 'as you know we have a very important job to do. Sometimes it is best not to worry but to have faith that if God wants us to do something important he will look after us so that we can do it.'

'I hope you are right,' said Abu Bakr.

It wasn't long before they heard the approach of the soldiers. With a clattering of weapons the soldiers got nearer to the cave and as they did so their voices got louder.

'Get your weapons ready men,' said one of them. 'They are probably hiding in this cave. If they are we'll soon find them.'

The soldiers got right up to the mouth of the cave and then stopped. Mohammed and Abu Bakr crouched silently in the darkness at the back of the cave.

'No point in going in there is there?' said one soldier.

'No,' said another, 'with that across the entrance they couldn't possibly have got in there without breaking it.'

Soon the sounds of movement started again, then—silence. Waiting a little longer Mohammed and Abu Bakr crept to the entrance of the cave. The soldiers were now out of sight but there stretched tightly across the entrance of the cave, and covering every part, was a beautiful, unbroken spider's web.

That night the two men were able to continue their journey to Medina.

47. It Happened One Christmas

St. Malo is a town in France. It is at the mouth of a river. Hundreds of years ago boatmen brought cargoes of wood down this river from forests. The wood was used by the people of St. Malo to make fires for warmth and cooking.

In the winter months, when most wood was needed, thick cold fogs often covered the river making the boat journey difficult and dangerous. But the boatmen got help. In the middle of the river was an island and on this island lived a man called Brother Johannick. When the fogs thickened Brother Johannick took a bell to the shores of his island and rang it day and night.

The boatmen, steering their heavily laden boats down the swirling river, heard the bell and knew where they were. They were all grateful to Brother Johannick for guiding them in the fog. To show their gratitude they threw bundles of logs and firewood from their boats as they passed the island. This wood drifted near the shore and Brother Johannick dragged it from the water and kept a warm fire ablaze with it.

The years passed by and the old man of the island got older. His beard was now snow white, his back was bent and it took him much longer to drag the heavy wood ashore. Then came a winter colder and bleaker than any before.

All through December Johannick rang his bell as frost and fog blanketed the river. By the time it was Christmas Eve the old man was very, very tired. Then, when he thought that Christmas Eve was passing to Christmas Day he knelt down to say a prayer on this most special of days.

As he knelt there, praying, the old man slowly sank to the ground. His bell stood silent beside him, and his fire dwindled away until it died out completely. There, on the frost covered island the thick fog lay over the exhausted old man.

Meanwhile one of the boatmen, safely ashore in his house, thought of Brother Johannick on his island.

'Poor old fellow,' thought Père Suliac. 'He's been ringing that bell for weeks. Now it's Christmas . . . I wonder if he's got enough firewood to keep him warm . . . I wonder if he is all right . . . I wonder . . .'

Père Suliac couldn't rest. Leaving his warm fireside he went down to the river, loaded his boat and pushed it out into the icy water. No sooner was he afloat than the peeling bell began to sound from the island.

'Hmmm,' thought the boatman, 'he sounds all right.'

Then as he rowed towards the sound of the bell, he noticed a strange bright light over the island. It was almost as if he was being guided there. Pulling strongly on the oars Père Suliac headed for the shore and then turned to let his boat drift into the shallower water. As he did so he saw an amazing sight.

The light showed Brother Johannick lying on the ground beside the embers of his once warm fire. It also showed a small child standing ringing the bell beside the old man.

Père Suliac had the most wonderful feeling of joy and happiness as he pulled the boat ashore, unloaded his firewood and waded up the beach with it. Dropping it on the ashes of the fire he knelt before the child to say a prayer . . . and . . . when he opened his eyes the light and the child were gone, but the fire blazed and Brother Johannick was standing there with the bell in his hand.

It was a Christmas neither man ever forgot.

48. A Play-mate's Doom

A throb of engines,
The whirr of propellers,
The sound of a knife-like bow
Cutting through the uneasy foam.

Splash!
Gurgling bubbles ease upwards;
A companion, a play-mate,
Now dead.

The trace of blood excites me.
Silence is then broken by the throb,
The whirr,
The cries of joy.

And now I'm solitary,
Morale declines,
Spirit drained,
I'm still alive; yet dead.

Philip Leighton (aged 12)

49. The Fight against the Serpent

The river lay still under the baking heat. Dead fish floated on its surface, some cows who had drunk the poisoned water lay dying on the bank and the villagers looked on fearfully and uncertain. A terrible serpent had come to live in the river and had killed everything in and near it.

Now it so happened that in order to try and rid the world of evil the great god Vishnu had disguised himself as a young boy called Krishna and came to live in the village near this river. Krishna knew that the serpent was Kaliya, one of the most powerful of all the forces of evil.

'I've got to do something to help these poor people,' said Krishna to his half-brother Rama. 'After all that is why I am here.'

So saying he climbed carefully along the branch of a dead tree which swept low over the river. Then, taking a deep breath, he dived in. At once the river erupted in bubbling, thrashing movements. Kaliya, furious at being disturbed, attacked at once.

For several minutes boy and creature writhed round each other. Startled by the noise the villagers raced from their houses and lined the river banks. Scarcely daring to hope they watched the struggle until suddenly Kaliya's coils encircled Krishna and he lost consciousness.

'We must help!' several of the villagers cried out.

'Yes—now, we must jump in.'

'No!'

The voice of Rama suddenly boomed out. 'Wait,' he cried.

Then turning back to the river he called out again.

'Krishna, have you forgotten who you are and why you are here? We need your help.'

Through his pain Krishna heard his half-brother's cry and at once twisted suddenly free from Kaliya's grip. Surging to the surface he leapt onto the serpent's head and forced him to submit.

'Now,' he cried, 'your place is far out in the sea where you cannot harm man. Go there at once and never again return to rivers like this.'

When the serpent had gone the river became pure again and served the needs of the villagers. Krishna had done his work well.

adapted from Mahabharata

50. Easter

In the white dust of Jerusalem
God laughed and walked and spoke
In pictures and in parables
To scores of common folk.

In the green grove of Gethsemane
God feared and prayed and wept
Upon the ground great drops of blood
While John and Peter slept.

On the grey hill of Calvary
God stretched His arms out wide.
Torn by the nails and racked by thirst
He broke His heart and died.

In the dim Easter garden
God's broken body lay.
He cast aside the swaddling bands
And rose at break of day.

What was it *for*, this Passion?
Why should it haunt us still
That one man out of millions
Was tortured on a hill?

God tried, two thousand years ago,
In agony tried He,
To copy the humanity
That patterns you and me.

For loneliness and cruelty,
For sorrow, pain and fear
Are not unusual things to feel
For us whose home is here.

And yet the God reminds us—
The seed within the earth
Dies to let the shoot go forth—
That death's the way to birth.

Monica Furlong

51. The Power of Prayer

The year that Mohammed was born was a terrifying one for the Arabs who lived in the city of Mecca. For some time they had feared attack from Abraha and the powerful army from Abyssinia. Now news reached the city that the attack was under way.

At the time the people's leader in Mecca was a man called Abd-al-Muttalib. When he heard the frightening news of the forthcoming attack he gathered all the people together.

'We know,' he said, 'that Abraha's army is far too strong for us to fight. We must seek to be saved by other ways.'

Then he gave his people instructions of what to do. He sent them out of the city to the hills surrounding it. Finally, alone in the silent city, Abd-al-Mattalib stood before the sacred temple, the Kaaba, and prayed. In his prayers he asked that since any man would seek to protect his own house, would God not now protect *his* own house, the Kaaba? His prayers ended, Abd-al-Mattalib joined the rest of his people on the hilltops.

They had not long to wait before the attacking army came into sight. They knew immediately that it was Abraha because leading the army was a creature of terrifying size. This was an elephant, something the Arabs had heard of but never seen before.

With his troops at the ready Abraha followed the great elephant into the city. Then a strange thing happened. As soon as the elephant was within the boundaries of the city it stopped. The soldiers following prodded it to keep it moving.

The elephant, however, stood quite still, and then slowly it knelt down. At a signal from their commander the soldiers clubbed and beat the huge animal. It remained unmoved.

It was obvious to the watching Arabs that this strange action had caused Abraha and his men to become uneasy. Eventually several of the soldiers managed to drag the elephant round until it was facing away from the city. Immediately it stood up and began to walk away. After a moment or two's uncertainty Abraha and his troops followed it. Mecca had been saved.

52. The World in a Hand

'I'm clever, I learn things quickly, I can get people to do what I want—there is no reason why I shouldn't get to be the most important person in the world.'

So thought a certain monkey. He certainly was clever and he did become important enough to rule over others and make their lives difficult with his boastful ways.

Soon the Lord Buddha heard about this and he decided he would have to investigate.

'Now my friend,' he said to the monkey. 'I hear you are a very important person.'

'Oh yes,' replied the monkey. 'What's more I am going to become the most important person in the world.'

'Hmm,' answered the Buddha, 'are you important and clever enough to jump out of my hand?'

The monkey stared at the Buddha.

'Out of your hand—why that would be ridiculously easy for me.'

'There you are then,' said the Buddha, stretching out his hand.

The monkey stepped onto it and then, closing his eyes, he flung himself upwards and outwards as far as he could. For ages and ages he seemed to hurtle through space and then he landed. Gasping with astonishment he found that he was right at the edge of the world. There was nothing between him and space except for five tall pillars.

'What a jump,' thought the monkey to himself, 'but how am I going to prove to the Buddha that I have jumped so far?'

Then he had an idea. He scratched a mark on one of the pillars so that he could bring the Buddha to see it. Then, closing his eyes again he launched himself back in the direction he had come from. After what seemed like another very long time he found himself back on the Buddha's hand again. He opened his eyes.

'Well,' smiled the Buddha, 'you've done a great deal of hopping about on my hand—but when are you going to leave it?'

'Leave it!' cried the monkey. 'I have already jumped from it to the end of the world, and what's more I can prove it.'

'Oh!'

'Yes,' said the monkey. 'There were five pillars there and I put a mark on one of them to show that I had been there.'

At this the Lord Buddha smiled and lifted up the fingers and thumb of his hand. On one of the fingers was the scratch the monkey had made.

53. Maya

Hindus believe that life on earth is not really 'real' at all but is like a sort of dream, which they call maya. However, whilst we are alive on earth all we really know is the maya.

Now there was once a famous holy man called Narada. Narada worried about knowing only maya and one day the great god Vishnu appeared in front of him.

'Narada,' said Vishnu, 'I have come to ask you a favour. Will you get me some water please?'

At the time both Narada and Vishnu were standing in the middle of a burning hot desert. In the distance could just be seen the outline of a village.

'Certainly Lord,' replied Narada, and set off towards the village.

Soon he reached the nearest house and knocked on the door. He was very hot and tired. A beautiful girl answered the door and when Narada saw the cool and inviting room inside he completely forgot what he had come for. Once inside the house he was warmly greeted by the rest of the girl's family and he soon felt very much at home.

Time seemed to go by quickly and pleasantly and before many months had passed Narada asked the head of the family if he could marry his daughter. By now she and Narada had become very fond of each other.

Everybody seemed pleased at the thought of the wedding and when it took place it was a happy occasion. So Narada settled down to life in the village. Eventually his father-in-law died and he became head of the family. By now he had three children and was busy managing a large estate.

Then, after twelve years, the rainy season was an unusually violent one. The river rose in its banks until one night it burst over the top and flood waters poured into the village. Desperately Narada tried to save his family. Clinging onto his wife and children he struggled to reach higher ground but a sudden surge of water swept them away from him. Then the pounding of the waters knocked him unconscious. When he recovered he found himself lying on a rock. All round him lay thick, muddy water. There was not a living creature in sight. Narada covered his face with his hands and began to cry.

'Narada.'

He suddenly heard the voice behind him. Opening his eyes he turned and saw the god Vishnu standing there. There was no flood, no swirling water—only the burning desert.

'I have been waiting half an hour for that water I asked you to bring,' said Vishnu.

Narada gasped and opened his mouth. Before he could speak however, Vishnu smiled and went on.

'But I see you have discovered the secret of maya.'

54. Giving

Arap Sang was old, tired and hot. As he walked along in the heat of the sun he felt worn out and looked for some shade. Presently he saw a vulture.

'Ah, Vulture,' he said, 'would you spread your wings and let me sit in the shade of them for a while.'

'No', said the vulture, 'I haven't got time for that sort of thing,' and flew away.

Soon Arap Sang came to an elephant.

'Elephant,' he said. 'I am finding it too hot to walk. Will you open your ears and let me walk beside you in their shade?'

'No,' said the elephant. 'I've got a headache and I want to get into some proper shade. I can't be bothered to walk as slowly as you do.'

Arap Sang walked and soon he came to a flock of cranes.

'Birds, Birds,' said the old man. 'Will you gather round me and open your wings? Then I can sit in their shade for a while until I feel better.'

'Certainly,' said the cranes as they gathered round the old man. Now Arap Sang had magic powers and when he felt better he spoke again to the cranes.

'You are the kindest creatures I have met today,' he said. 'I am going to give you each something which will remind you and everybody else how kind you are.'

Then Arap Sang touched each bird. As he did so a golden crown grew on each head.

Some time later Arap Sang was at his house when, with a fluttering of tired wings, a crane dragged itself towards him. Arap Sang was shocked as he saw the state of the bird. It's feathers were torn and broken and it was desperately sad.

'Your gift, Arap Sang, your gift—please take it away'.

'What?' gasped the old man.

'These crowns you gave us', went on the bird. 'Everywhere men now hunt us and kill us so that they can get the crowns.'

'My friend', said Arap Sang, 'I can't tell you how sorry I am. How foolish it was for me to make a gift of something which has caused you nothing but distress. what is the good of a gift like that?'

Then the old man touched the bird again. The gold crown disappeared and in its place came some of the most beautiful feathers ever seen. Now the crane wears a crown of beautiful feathers rather than gold but he is still called the crowned crane.

55. What Did You Expect?

The two old men bent their heads forward as they talked together.

'It was like this,' said old Suvil. 'I was so ill that I thought I was going to die, and so did everybody else. So I shared out all my money between my sons—and then I got better. Since then my life has been miserable. I have no money of my own, none of my sons want to be bothered with me in their houses and their wives begrudge me even a decent meal.'

'Ah my friend,' said the other old man. 'Why don't you try this . . . ?'

When he had finished speaking Suvil's tired old face broke into a gentle smile.

Next day, at one of his son's houses a man arrived with a heavy looking bag for Suvil. The old man put it under his bed and said nothing about it. When he moved to another son's house for a few days he took the bag with him. Whilst he was there, another bag arrived for him.

Then a mysterious rumour began to go round the neighbourhood. Somebody who had owed Suvil a great deal of money was paying it off to him a bag at a time.

Suddenly Suvil's sons couldn't do enough for him. It was 'Welcome Father, can I get anything for you? Where would you like to go?' Their wives began to make him tasty meals. No longer was the old man neglected and he lived in peace and comfort.

Then, a few years later he died. After the sorrowing for his death was over the sons rushed back to the bags under his bed. Quickly they emptied them out onto the floor to find—they were all full of pebbles and stones.

56. Being Too Clever

When the monkey got a thorn caught in his tail he could not pull it out.

'This is a nuisance,' he said to himself and went to see a barber.

'Could you help me to get this thorn out please?' he asked the barber.

'Well, I'll try,' replied the barber, 'keep quite still.'

Very carefully he managed to get the thorn out but as he did so he made a small cut on the monkey's tail.

'Aha,' thought the monkey, 'I'll make the most of this.'

'Oh, oh,' he wailed, 'You've cut me, you've cut me. Get rid of that cut at once.'

Of course the barber couldn't get rid of the cut he had made and the monkey went on making a terrible fuss. Finally to shut him up the barber gave him one of his razors.

Well pleased the sly monkey went off. Soon he saw an old woman cutting some wood.

'Here's my chance to be clever again,' he thought.

Going up to the old woman he offered her his razor to help cut the wood. The old woman didn't think it would be much good but she didn't want to appear ungrateful to this kind monkey. No sooner had she started to cut with the razor than it broke.

'My razor,' howled the monkey. 'It's the only thing I own and now its broken. Oh what am I to do?'

Well, to quieten him down, the old woman gave the monkey all the wood she had cut.

'This is getting better,' thought the monkey and soon he came across a man who was cooking fish cakes on a fire. Now the monkey was very hungry.

He sat down beside the man and started talking to him. As the fire died down the monkey threw his firewood on it to keep it going. Suddenly he pretended that he had just noticed all his firewood was gone.

'Oh dear,' he cried, 'my wood . . . it's all gone. Now I won't be able to cook my meal. I'll be hungry and I've no food and . . .'

He went on so much that the man gave him all his cooked fish cakes.

'Oh, I'm clever all right,' said the monkey to himself as he dashed away with the fish cakes. 'I deserve the feast I'm going to have.'

No sooner had he thought that, than a pack of wild dogs leapt out of the trees at him. They had smelt the fish cakes. The monkey was terrified, dropped the fish cakes and fled up the nearest tree. The dogs enjoyed them!

57.   Is It Worth It?

One day Nasrudin and his wife had a terrible argument. It started off because neither of them wanted to feed the donkey. After arguing and arguing about it they finally came to a ridiculous agreement. Neither of them would speak—and the first one who broke this agreement would have to feed the donkey.

All day they moved about the house in silence. The only noise came from outside where the poor donkey brayed long and loud for his breakfast . . . his lunch . . . anything!

Eventually Nasrudin's wife could stand the silence no longer. She went out of the house and crossed the road to see her friend. Once her husband couldn't hear she decided it was safe to speak.

'Oh' she said to her neighbour, 'he's such a stubborn man. He'll do anything to avoid speaking first . . . and I'm not going to let him. What should I do?'

'I know,' said the neighbour. 'We have just made some lovely soup. I'll send my son over with a bowl. I know how Nasrudin loves his food.'

So the neighbour went to prepare a bowl of soup.

Meanwhile strange things were happening in Nasrudin's house. A thief had broken in. He took everything worth stealing—and then he came to the room where Nasrudin was sitting in the middle of the floor. Now Nasrudin had heard the thief but he realised he would have to speak if he chased him or tried to capture him. He wasn't going to speak!

Then he decided he would sit quite still and not move a muscle when the thief came into the room. Well, of course, the thief got a terrible shock when he saw a man sitting there. Then when he noticed that the man was not moving he thought he must be in some kind of trance—and he was wearing a beautiful turban. Snatching the turban from Nasrudin's head the thief dashed out into the street and made off with his loot.

No sooner had he left than the neighbour's son arrived with the soup. As soon as Nasrudin saw him he pointed to the cupboards emptied by the thief and then, still not speaking of course, he pointed to his head over and over again.

The neighbour's son watched all this in amazement.

'He's mad, this Nasrudin,' he thought to himself, 'but he obviously wants me to pour this soup over his head—so I'd better do it.'

This he did and the soup poured down Nasrudin's head and face and ran over his clothes onto the carpet. At this moment his wife came back to see what was happening. She saw the empty cupboards, the empty shelves where her precious ornaments should have been, and her husband covered in soup.

'In the name of Allah . . .' she cried out.

'Ah,' said Nasrudin. 'You spoke first. I've won!'

adapted from *Folk Tales of Turkey* by S. Dhar

58.   A Foolish Move

Two farmers met one day and began talking.

'I must say your farm seems to be doing very well,' said Jacob.

'Oh yes,' said Ben. 'In fact I'm getting richer and richer. Some people wouldn't know what to do with all this wheat I'm growing and all this money I'm making.'

'Is that so?' said Jacob.

'Yes it is,' continued Ben. 'But I know what to do with it my friend, I can tell you.'

'Hmm,' said Jacob.

'You see over there,' went on Ben. 'I'm going to build one of the biggest barns you've ever seen. It will be so big that I can store all my wheat and all my riches in it. I won't have to give anything away or sell anything cheap. I'll be rich for ever more, I won't need to work hard. I'll just be able to sit back and look at my huge barn packed with all those good things, and then enjoy myself.

'Hmm,' said Jacob.

The days passed into weeks and work on the enormous barn began. Soon it could be seen from all over the countryside. Then when the building was finished Ben's workers began to pack it with all the things which were going to keep him rich for life. Finally, everything was completed. The huge barn was packed full of riches. That night Ben died in his sleep.

adapted from the Bible

59. Think First—or Last?

Out on the prairie it was snowing. Leaping through the snow, throwing up a trail behind him was the Hare.

The Fox saw him coming.

'What's the matter, Hare?' called Fox.

'Can't stop,' gasped Hare as he flashed by.

'Oh dear,' thought the Fox as he saw the Hare vanishing into the distance. 'Oh dear, something must be wrong—I'd better be moving!'

The Fox began racing through the snow as fast as he could go. A Wolf saw him coming.

'What is it, why are you running like that?' shouted the Wolf.

'Can't stop,' gasped the Fox as he rushed by.

'Whatever he's running from must be dangerous,' thought the Wolf to himself. 'I'd better move quickly.'

The Wolf raced away through the snow. A Bear saw him coming.

'Wolf, Wolf, what's the matter? What are you running from?'

The Wolf saw the Bear out of the corner of his eye.

'Can't stop, must get away,' he muttered as he gasped for breath.

'Hmm,' thought the Bear. 'I'm bigger and stronger than he is but if he is running away as fast as that . . . hmm . . . I'd better be going!' So the Bear lumbered off through the woods.

Meanwhile the Hare was exhausted. He stopped and sat gasping in the snow. suddenly he was aware of a noise behind him. Turning he saw Fox coming to a stop. A short while later Wolf joined them and then, just when they were getting their breath back up came Bear.

'Well?' said Bear to Wolf.

'Well?' said Wolf to Fox.

'Well?' said Fox to Hare.

'What do you mean "Well"?' said Hare. 'I was sitting under a tree when a huge lump of snow fell off and nearly hit me. I got such a fright I ran and ran and ran.'

'Why . . .' said Fox.

'. . . you, . . .' said Wolf.

'. . . silly, . . .' said Bear.

'No, no,' said Hare. 'I don't think I'm the one who is silly here.'

60. Be Content

There was once a holy man who lived beside the great sacred River Ganges. His home was a simple hut and his only companion was a tiny mouse. This mouse was a grumbler. One day it spoke to the holy man.

'Sir,' it said, 'I thank you for all the scraps of food you bring me, but when you are out I am terrified a cat will come and eat me. Will you not make me into a cat?'

The holy man looked at his tiny mouse friend.

'Very well,' he said, and changed the mouse into a cat.

A few days went by and then, one evening as the holy man was feeding his cat, the creature said to him, 'Sir, when you are out my life is very difficult. Packs of wild dogs come near the hut and I am afraid they will catch me and tear me to pieces. Could you make me into a dog?'

The holy man smiled, and changed his companion into a dog.

Afer a few days, as he put down a meal for the dog, it looked up at him and said, 'Sir, it is so kind of you to feed me like this but if I was an ape you would not need to. I could swing in the trees and get my own food when I wanted it.'

So the holy man changed the dog into an ape. Well, after a short time went by the ape wanted to be changed into a wild boar. No sooner was it a wild boar than it wanted to be an elephant.

So the holy man's little mouse was now an elephant. Crashing through the jungle one day it was seen by the king. He had it captured and prepared specially to carry his queen. The elephant wasn't too keen on this and one day it misbehaved so badly that the queen was thrown off and hurt. The elephant escaped into the jungle. It made its way back to the holy man.

'Sir,' it said, 'it was dreadful having to carry humans on my back. Now I am in trouble as well, and you should have seen the fuss the king made over that queen. Can you not change me from an elephant to a human. I don't want to be ordinary though—I want to be a queen.'

'Ah,' said the holy man, 'I can't do that because you can only become a queen by marrying a king. However, I will turn you into a beautiful lady.'

Well one day the beautiful lady was sitting outside the holy man's hut when a finely dressed man came by. He had lost his way in a hunt. After she had given him a meal and looked after him the man said that he was a king, and asked the beautiful lady to marry him.

She did and went to live in a magnificent palace. Shortly after this, however, she slipped, fell into a large tank of water in the palace grounds, and drowned.

61. Thank You or . . .

Once there was a fisherman who worked long and hard catching only a few fish in his basket traps. One day as he pulled in his baskets one of them seemed very heavy.

'Aah, good luck at last,' thought the fisherman, 'with a weight as heavy as this I must have got a really good catch.'

Struggling with all his might he heaved the basket on board his small boat and found inside it—an old woman!

'Thank you kind Sir,' said the old woman. 'If you take me home to live with you, you won't regret it.'

'But,' gasped the fisherman, 'I work very hard and I can only barely make enough to keep myself alive.'

'Just do as I say and you'll live to be thankful,' said the old woman.

So the fisherman took the old woman to his home. 'After all', he thought to himself, 'I can hardly be much worse off than I am now.'

No sooner had the two got to the fisherman's hut than the old woman said, 'Now build a strong fence round the ground next to your hut. Put a gate in it but leave the gate open.'

The fisherman was astonished but there was something about the old woman which made him do as she said.

Next morning when he got up he was flabbergasted. Inside the fence was a huge herd of cattle and the gate was firmly shut behind them.

'Well . . . ,' said the fisherman, 'a man with a herd of cattle like this is a rich man indeed.'

And so it was. The poor fisherman became one of the richest men around. No longer did he have to sweat and strain in his tiny boat. Now he could go round to the villages and talk to people and say the sort of things he thought important men should say.

Unfortunately as time went by he got more and more lazy and foolish. He spent most of his time telling people what he thought they should do and he became more and more fed up of the old woman from the sea who still lived with him.

One night he came home and said, 'An important man like me should be able to have just who he wants in his house. I'm tired of having you here.'

The old woman stood up and walked out of the house. When she had passed through the gate of the fence all the cattle then followed her. As the man watched, the woman and cattle disappeared in the direction of the sea—and were never seen again.

The next day, having learnt his lesson too late, the man dragged his boat down to the shore and started fishing again. For the rest of his life he was what he had been before—a very poor fisherman.

62. The More We Know

There is a very old story which has been told for about seven hundred years. It shows that if we only took the trouble to find out the proper facts what a lot of arguments could be avoided. Well, this old story goes like this:

There were once four men and they were given some money to spend between them. Now one of these four men was a Greek and he said, 'I want to spend this money on Stafil.'

'Nonsense,' said the second man, 'I want to use the money to buy Inab.'

Now the second man was an Arab and no sooner had he finished speaking than the third man, who was a Persian, sprang to his feet.

'I don't know what you are talking about,' he said, 'but this money should be spent on Angur.'

All this time the fourth man had just been listening to what was going on. Like the others, he understood some, but not all of what was being said. Finally he got to his feet, pushed the others aside and said in a very important voice, 'This money should be spent on Uzum.'

The fourth man was a Turk and when he said this the others all began to shout again about what they wanted the money spent on. Soon they started to fight.

This was all a great pity for the Greek word 'Stafil', the Arabic word 'Inab', the Persian word 'Angur', and the Turkish word 'Uzum' all meant the same thing! Each man wanted some grapes.

63. What Cannot Be Changed

Three men were out hunting one day and they had with them a young boy. One of the men, Ali, was a great hunter and very proud of his skill with the bow. Ahmad was thought of as a very wise man and people from all around came to him for advice when they were ill or hurt in any way. Sayad, the third man, said little but thought a lot.

As they moved slowly through the trees Ali had his bow drawn ready to fire an arrow instantly.

'Are we likely to find anything here?' Ahmad asked in a whisper.

'Yes, animals are usually to be found in this place,' replied Ali, 'as long as we move as silently as possible.'

'Where is the boy?' asked Sayad.

'Oh, he's around somewhere,' said Ali.

At that moment there was a sudden flurry in some bushes.

'There—what is it?' cried Ahmad.

Even as Ahmad spoke Ali sent his arrow winging towards the bush. Then, to the horror of the three men there was a cry and the boy fell from the bush to the ground. As the men rushed towards the injured boy, Ali, without thinking, shouted at Ahmad.

'You fool, it's all your fault. If you hadn't cried out I wouldn't have fired. If this boy is dead you will be to blame.'

At this Ahmad stopped, and without another word, walked away.

'He's hurt badly,' said Ali as they reached the boy. 'We need Ahmad, he's an expert in dealing with injured people.'

'But he has gone,' replied Sayad. 'You must follow quickly to catch him and bring him back.'

'Not I,' said Ali.

Desperately the two men tried to save the injured boy's life but it was no use. As they sadly stood together afterwards Sayad said, 'This is a tragic lesson. Three things cannot be brought back once they have taken place—the fired arrow, the hasty and thoughtless word, and the missed opportunity.

adapted from *The Caravan of Dreams* by I. Shah

64. What We See in Others

Brahma, chief of the gods, looked closely at the others who were gathered round him.

'Well,' said Brahma to the other gods, 'we have spent a long time visiting Earth and seeing how these humans behave.'

'Yes, yes,' replied another of the gods. 'There is certainly a great deal of room for their improvement.'

Brahma continued.

'I agree, and that is why I have planned the gift I have told you about. Perhaps when Man understands what to do with it he will become a better person.'

'You're right,' answered another god. 'Let us bring him in now and give him our present.'

So Man was brought before the gods.

'Now,' said Brahma, 'we have a gift for you. It is made up of two sacks.'

'What is it?' asked Man.

'One sack has in it all your own faults,' went on Brahma.

Man looked very dissatisfied at this.

'What about the other sack?' he said.

'That one contains all the faults of your neighbours,' replied Brahma.

So Man was given the two sacks and the gods disappeared. When left by himself Man looked at the gift and stroked his chin in thought. Then he made his decision.

Picking up the sack with his own faults in it, he threw it unopened over his shoulder so that he could not even see it. Then, with a smile, he opened the sack with his neighbours' faults in and walked along with it held in front of him. He looked in it regularly smiling slyly as he did so.

High above the gods looked down and shook their heads. They are still waiting for Man to change.

adapted from *Folk Tales of Sri Lanka* by M. Ratnatunga

65. The Greedy Fox

There was once a fox who lived beside a great lake. He spent many of his days watching the gulls flying over the lake—and wondering where their nests were!

One day he was lucky. Creeping through some rushes near the shore of the lake he almost fell over a gull's nest—and there in it were some newly born babies.

'Aah,' said the fox. 'This is my lucky day. I'll take these home for dinner.'

Quickly he bundled up the chicks and set off for home. On the way though he kept thinking.

'This is my lucky day. Why don't I make the most of it? There must be loads more nests near here. I'll just put my bundle down and have a quick look round. Then, instead of just a nice dinner I might be able to have a real feast.'

As the fox was sniffing through the rushes the gull, who had returned to her nest and found her babies missing, flew overhead. Seeing the bundle lying on the ground she swooped down, and almost cried with relief when she found her babies safe and sound inside.

'Now to teach that fox a lesson,' she said and filled the bundle with thorns and sharp stones. No sooner had she done this than the fox returned.

He was not in a very good mood. He had not found any more nests and this had annoyed him.

I'm going to eat my dinner right here and now,' he said and plunged his paw into the bundle. Immediately he let out a howl of pain and looking at his paw saw that it was full of thorns.

Now, in an instant he knew what had happened and he looked quickly round. He was just in time to see the gull, who had just hidden her babies carefully, flying towards the lake. Like a flash of lightning the fox leapt after her. Jumping up he just failed to reach and then—they came to the waters of the lake.

The gull flew out a little way and then came down to settle on the surface of the water. The fox was furious. As he watched the gull bobbing slowly up and down he was sure the gull was laughing at him.

'Grrr,' he thought to himself, grinding his teeth together in anger. 'If I wait here to catch that gull I could be here all day. There's only one thing to do, I'll drink all this water and then I'll get her.'

So the fox began to drink, and drink, and drink. Eventually he drank so much that he burst, and the gull and her family went safely home.

66. Look in the Right Direction

Ever since he was very young Gamini had always been interested in looking at the night sky. He studied the stars, the patterns they made, the distance away they seemed to be. Gradually he became an expert on stars and people respected his opinions.

After a time, however, Gamini began to talk less and less about normal everyday things and more and more about stars. Far from asking his opinion now people tried to keep out of his way. To be trapped in conversation with him was to be bored with endless talk about nothing but stars. He never listened to what other people said and he thought only of his own interest.

One night Gamini was out in the village as usual. He wandered round the streets gazing upwards all the time at the sky above. Now it so happened that a deep drain had been dug at one end of the village.

'Gamini,' shouted a passing villager, 'be careful where you're walking round the next corner.'

Gamini ignored the shout and carried on looking skywards. Another villager passed by.

'Gamini,' he called out. 'There has been some very deep digging going on. You had better watch where you are going.'

'How bright they are tonight,' muttered Gamini to himself. 'How very bright.'

He continued along the main path through the village until he reached the deep ditch. Continuing to stare upwards he did not see the ditch until his feet felt the ground end and he plunged downwards. Immediately he was plunged into a deep, watery mess. The sides of the ditch were so steep and shiny that he could not get out; he gasped as his head ached from the blow he had received. At last he got his breath back.

'Help!' he cried. 'Somebody please help me.'

The two villagers who had passed him were not surprised to hear the cries. Running back they soon managed to haul Gamini to safety.

'I hope you've learned a lesson tonight,' murmured one of them as he hauled the frightened and bruised Gamini out of the ditch.

67. Don't Try to Be What You Are Not

In the middle of a large forest lived a lion. One day a jackal came by. The lion was kind and let the jackal stay. This suited the jackal very much because he was able to feast on the flesh of animals which the lion had killed.

Days went by and the jackal got fatter and very pleased with himself.

'Don't call me "Jackal" any more,' he said to the lion.

'Indeed,' replied the lion. 'What shall I call you then?'

'What about "Small Lion"?' said the jackal.

'As you wish,' went on the lion. 'From now on you will be "Small Lion".'

More days went by and the jackal got more and more proud of himself. As he and the lion were eating together he spoke again.

'I'm tired of being called "Small Lion",' he said. 'I want to be called something else now.'

'Oh,' replied the lion. 'What is it to be this time then?'

'I want to be called "Great Lion",' replied the jackal.

'Ah, there's only one problem there. If you want to be called that you'll have to be able to roar like a lion.'

'That's not going to be a problem,' replied the foolish jackal.

Next day he was out in the forest and he saw an elephant. Stopping in front of the huge creature he opened his mouth to roar like a lion.

Surprised at the foolishness of this jackal who stood yelping in front of him, the elephant lifted one great foot and kicked him aside. The jackal died for his stupidity.

68. What Others Say

A group of Kadambawa men were making a long journey. On their second night on the road they stopped, had their evening meal and then settled down for the night. Whilst he was asleep one of them had a dream about an elephant.

The next day he told the others about the dream. One of the men who listened thought that he was very clever at saying what dreams meant.

'Oh yes,' he said, when the dreamer had finished. 'That definitely means bad news. Where there is an elephant there is rice, where there is rice must be a village. Your dream means something has happened at our village. It must be bad—we must go back at once.'

So, very worried and upset about what might have happened at their village, the Kadambawa men set off on the return journey. They travelled as fast as they could.

When they got nearly home the women and boys of the village saw them coming. Immediately one woman cried out.

'Look, look, the men are returning. They should not have been back yet. Something is wrong!'

So all the women in the village began to cry and shout aloud because they thought something was terribly wrong.

Meanwhile the Kadambawa men had almost reached the outskirts of the village when they heard the terrible crying.

'Aaah,' said the man who thought he knew what dreams meant. 'You see— there is trouble here. Listen to that crying. It is a good thing we have come home.'

So the women rushed out to meet the men, and the men put their arms round the women to console them. There was a great deal of crying—and no explanations.

Meanwhile a passing traveller heard the noise. He stepped into the main path of the village.

'What is wrong? Who is dead here?' he cried out.

Hearing the questions the Kadambawa men and women stopped their shouting and crying and asked each other the same questions. No-one was dead and nothing dreadful had happened to anybody. They went shame-faced to their houses as the stranger went on his way.

adapted from *Village Folk Tales of Ceylon* by H. Parker

69. We Must Understand

A deaf man was ploughing a rice field when a traveller stopped near him.

'Can you tell me how far it is to the nearest city?' asked the traveller.

'I got this bull from my father-in-law,' replied the deaf man.

The traveller looked amazed.

'I don't want to know about your bull my friend, I just want to know the way.'

'Don't argue with me about my bull,' said the deaf man, and pushed the traveller away from him.

That night the deaf man went home. He spoke to his wife.

'Do you know a man stopped me working today and started arguing about my bull. Would you believe it!'

The wife, who was also deaf, spoke sharply to her husband.

'I've had a job to find firewood and water and vegetables today. Your meal is going to be late.'

'Where is my food?' asked the deaf man.

'If you will just be patient your meal will soon be ready,' said the woman.

'Why is my food not here?' asked the deaf man.

They argued for the rest of the night.

adapted from *Village Folk Tales of Ceylon* by H. Parker

70. Sour Grapes

'They are just what I am looking for,' said the fox as he gazed at the hillside covered with large, juicy looking bunches of grapes.

Waiting until no-one else was around he then crept silently into the vineyard. Walking along the rows of vines he considered one bunch of grapes after another.

'Hmm,' he thought, as he stood in front of one particularly big bunch. 'These look the best. I'll have this bunch.'

There was just one snag however. The grapes were rather high up and the fox could not quite reach them. First he stood on his hind legs, then he crouched down and leapt upwards, then he looked for something to stand on. It was no use, he just couldn't reach the grapes.

'Ah well,' he said to himself, 'what does it matter, there are plenty of others to choose from.' So he set off to find himself another bunch.

Before long, however, the fox had made an unpleasant discovery. Not only could he not reach the bunches he fancied most, he couldn't reach any at all. He got more and more angry, stretching and leaping about without being able to get a single grape.

Finally he stormed out of the vineyard, talking to himself as he did.

'Hm,' he said, 'who would want to eat those grapes anyway. It's obvious that they are all sour and juiceless, I wouldn't want to eat them!'

adapted from Aesop

71. Making Your Mind Up

The magistrate looked severely at the thief who stood in front of him.

'You will of course be punished for your theft—but at least you will be able to choose the punishment.'

'Yes Lord,' replied the thief, lowering his head.

'As you are convicted of stealing food the punishment I give you is this. You will either eat one hundred onions, receive one hundred lashes, pay a fine of one hundred rupees—or go to prison.'

The thief thought for a minute. He could hardly believe his ears—what luck! There was no doubt which was the easiest of that lot.

'I will eat the onions lord,' he said.

Baskets of onions were brought and the man began his punishment. He crammed onion after onion into his mouth, crunching them as quickly as he could. One, two, three baskets emptied but by now the thief felt as if his throat was on fire. He eyes streamed, his nose ran and he felt so utterly miserable that he cried out.

'Stop, stop!' Nothing could be worse than this. 'I'll take the lashes.'

Quickly he was tied to a pillar and his back was bared. After only a few searing strokes, however, the thief cried out again.

'Enough, enough, the pain is unbearable. I'll pay the fine.'

And so the foolish man endured the onion eating, suffered the pain of the whipping and finally had to pay the 100 rupee fine—and the interest it cost him to borrow the money.

adapted from the *Panchantantra*

72. Fact or Fancy?

One night the Kadambawa men were taking their drums to another village. They were going there to sing and dance. As they moved along the forest track it got dark quickly.

Suddenly one of the men stopped.

'Look, look—up there just off the path.'

'What is it?' asked another.

'It's an elephant,' replied the first.

'He's right beside the path—he'll never let us get past.'

'Look he's moving. I can see his huge ears shaking from side to side.'

'You're right. What shall we do?'

So the Kadambawa men huddled together to decide what they should do. Finally they decided that the best thing would be to beat their drums. The noise might persuade the elephant to go away, and it would certainly stop him coming any nearer to them.

Out came the tom-toms and they began to beat away in the night. In the moonlight they could still see the elephant. Sometimes he shook his ears from side to side but apart from that he did not move.

The long hours of the night passed slowly. The Kadambawa men very much wanted to get on to the next village but they did not dare move, or stop playing their tom-toms.

Finally the first pale light of dawn streaked through the trees.

'Look, look . . .' said one of the drummers.

They all looked up the path towards the . . . it was not an elephant at all. A huge Wara bush leaned over the path and occasionally its giant leaves swayed from side to side.

The Kadambawa men had wasted the whole night.

adapted from *Village Folk Tales of Ceylon* by H. Parker

73. Pride Goes before a Fall

The first goose looked at the pool.

'In another few weeks it will have dried up completely,' he said.

'Yes,' replied the second goose. 'All those years we have lived here and now this happens.'

'Well, there's nothing else for it, we'll have to fly off and find a deeper pool.'

'Hey, just a minute,' another voice called and the two geese turned to see their friend the tortoise beside them.

'You know I've always lived beside this pool too—and we've always been good friends. If you leave I want you to take me with you.'

'But how can we?' asked the first goose. 'We'll be flying to look for a new home—you can't do that.'

'You don't think a problem like that would stop a clever person like me do you?' asked the tortoise. 'Now look, if you get a long stick and each of you holds one end in your mouth, I will hold on to the middle by my mouth.'

'But that's far too dangerous,' protested the second goose. 'You'd only have to open your mouth for a second and you would fall to your death.'

'I'm not stupid!' replied the tortoise.

So the geese found a long stick. Each of them took one end in their mouths, the tortoise bit firmly onto the middle and they set off.

Now they had to pass over a certain city on their flight and as they did so people poured out of their houses to see this strange sight.

'Look, look,' they cried, 'what a wonderful idea. I wonder who thought of that?'

The tortoise heard this and he couldn't bear the people down below not to know that it was he who had thought up this clever plan.

'It was my id . . .'

As soon as he opened his mouth he fell to his death.

adapted from the *Panchantantra*

74.   The Promise

'My people have suffered enough,' thundered the emperor. 'This creature must be dealt with once and for all!'

The princes and warriors of Japan who stood before the emperor nodded obediently. They knew that he was talking about a terrifying bird which was covered with sharp, protective metal and which had been swooping down to carry off children. To kill this vicious bird would be a great honour—but it would also be very dangerous.

Finally one of the young warriors—Yashimasa—stepped forward.

'My lord, I will do it,' he said.

'It will not be easy,' continued the emperor. 'First the bird's lair must be found—and it will be a dangerous opponent. Many have been killed trying to rid us of its terror.'

'The honour of saving our people from it will therefore be all the greater,' said Yashimasa, bowing low.

And so the young warrior, armed with the sharpest of arrows set off on his task. For months he ranged back and forth over some of Japan's most beautiful countryside. From beaches to mountains to valleys he sought the armoured bird.

Finally, Yashimasa arrived at a valley with a river running through it. By now he was very tired after his ceaseless searching and there he met, and soon fell in love with, a beautiful girl. The girl's name was Shiragika and soon she and Yashimasa were spending all their days together. The young warrior had almost forgotten about his task when one day he heard the terrifying sound of the metal-covered wings clanking overhead. Quickly he and Shiragika hid. They then saw the dreaded bird fly to its nest which was hidden in a tree near the river.

That night Yashimasa got his weapons and lay in wait for the bird. As dawn lit the sky the great creature launched itself from its nest. At once Yashimasa fired and his arrow hit the bird on the only part of its body which was not covered by armour. This was just below the heart and as the arrow struck home the bird fell dead with a terrible crash.

So Yashimasa told Shiragika that he must return to the emperor's palace with the news that the killer bird was dead.

'Will you come back?' asked Shiragika.

'Of course,' replied Yashimasa. 'I will return to marry you as soon as I can. I promise.'

When Yashimasa got back to the emperor's palace he was a hero. Great feasts were held in his honour and he was cheered wherever he went. The emperor said that with such a great warrior to call upon how could he ask anyone else to do his most dangerous tasks for him. So Yashimasa was popular, famous and busy—and back in the valley Shiragika waited for him.

The days passed into weeks and the weeks into months. Shiragika waited and

Yashimasa grew more famous and rich. His promise was forgotten. Then one day Shiragika decided that Yashimasa was never coming back. She was so unhappy that she put on her best kimono and walked into the river until it covered her head.

Then amongst all his splendours the news reached Yashimasa. At once a sadness greater than anything he had ever known before came over him. What were his honours and feasts worth now? Now he longed to be able to keep his promise—but it was too late.

adapted from *The Magic Book of Birds* by T. Haddon

75. Too Late to Learn

'Oh Mr. Rat,' said the frog. 'Please come and visit me.'

'How can I?' replied the rat. 'How can I get across the water?'

'It will be easy,' said the frog. 'If I tie you to me you'll be quite safe.'

So the frog tied the rat tightly to his own body and began to swim across the pond. When he was half-way across he decided it was time to put his plan into action.

'If I dive down now,' he thought, 'the rat will soon drown and I'll have a good meal.'

No sooner had he thought this than he plunged beneath the surface. The rat, suddenly realising what has happening put up a terrific struggle. The water of the pond bubbled as the two creatures thrashed and twisted about.

High above, a bird, which had been flying by, suddenly noticed the commotion below. Swooping down he saw what was going on, skimmed over the water, snatched both creatures into his mouth and enjoyed his best meal for a long while.

adapted from La Fontaine

76. Robbed

'Ah, what it is to be important!' sighed the mule as the men loaded the bags full of treasure onto his back.

'There must be enough money in these bags to make a king rich—and it's all being carried by me.'

The mule looked to his left where his friend was also being loaded up. The load this time was just heavy sacks of grain because his friend worked for a miller.

'Never mind,' called out the proud mule. 'One day you might get to carry really important things like me.' Then he gave rather a haughty laugh.

Soon the two mules were on their way. They were both going in the same direction and had to follow a long, twisting path through a wood. The mule carrying the treasure was soon a long way ahead.

'Not only do I carry important goods—but they are so much lighter than loads like grain! How my friend must wish he were me.'

Just at that moment, however, the bushes parted and out leapt a group of robbers. Seizing the mule they dragged him to the ground. He tried to put up a fight but the men hit him with heavy clubs, tore his precious load from his back and escaped off into the woods with it.

A few minutes later the other mule came plodding up the path. When he saw his bruised and battered friend he stopped to give what help he could. He didn't say much but as he was helping he thought that sometimes it was far better to be working for a miller than a rich merchant.

77. There Is Plenty of Time

One day Satan was discussing with another devil how they could do more evil in the world.

'One thing you will soon realise,' said Satan. 'Man has a terrific capacity for doing terrible things—all he needs is a little encouragement.'

'Why don't we spread the word that there is no God then?' asked the other devil.

'No, no Man would not believe that.'

The second devil thought for a while then he came up with another idea.

'Why don't we spread the rumour that there is no hell then? That will give Man plenty of opportunity for doing wrong without any need to worry about it.'

Satan shook his head.

'Man is not stupid, but your suggestions have given me a good idea. Go to earth and remind Man that there is a God, then remind him that there is hell too. But then tell him not to worry as he has plenty of time before he need concern himself about either. Then you'll see what trouble he can get into!'

78. A Stranger

In a foreign country
I wriggle from sorrow
As I didn't know
Where to go,
Where to stand.
I feel so lonely,
I feel so strange
My steps are hesitant
Along the foreign land
As I walk.
    People around me
Are talking happily
But they talk different

a different place
a different language

and I am in between.

Katerina Theoharous

79. A Feast For Some

There was once a kind man who enjoyed giving great feasts for his friends. Because he was rich he could afford lovely food and he prepared his feasts with great care. Then when he had decided what there would be to eat he sent out his invitations.

He had prepared a very special feast on one occasion and when it was quite ready he sent out his servants to tell all his guests that it was ready.   ·

When his servant got to the first guest he was very surprised to hear the man say to him, 'No I can't come.'

When the servant looked surprised the man went on.

'Well it's like this you see, I've just got some more land and I can't just leave it. I've got to go and look after it so I won't be able to come to the feast.'

The servant hurried on to the next guest.

'Oh I am sorry,' said this guest when the servant told him the feast was ready. 'But you see I've got to see to my animals at the moment. I've got such a lot and they need feeding and looking after and I've got some new ones . . .'

Without listening to the rest of these excuses the servant hurried on with his master's message. He was astonished when he spoke to the next guest.

'Oh there's not a chance that I can come,' said the guest. 'I've just got married so I won't be there.'

Having heard even more excuses the servant went back to his master and told him that his guests weren't coming.

At first, as he looked at the long tables prepared with beautiful food, the master was very angry indeed. Then, he turned to the servant and said, 'Go out into the town. Find those poor unfortunate people who are beggars or cripples or blind. Bring them all back here and let them eat their fill.'

adapted from the Bible

80. Why Did He Laugh?

'And you only want sixpence for him, Mr. Blaikie?'

The farmer nodded. His eyes, too close together, narrowed slightly. His face no longer wore its smile of good humour when he spoke.

'You've got the money?' he snapped. 'But of course you have! Or why would you be asking for the wee dog?' He stretched out his big hand and waited.

Davie hesitated. The sixpence in his pocket was a lot of money. It was everything he had—the sum of all his work for the past month. His father would be angry at first when he learned it had been spent. But when he caught sight of the wee dog, he would understand. Holding the pup in one hand, Davie dug his fingers into the pocket of his trousers. Slowly he withdrew the small silver coin and dropped it into the farmer's hand. Mr. Blaikie's crafty face was all smiles again.

'Mind you take good care of him!' He chuckled as he turned away. 'There will not be many like him in these parts.'

Suddenly he laughed again, just as he had laughed before. Davie could see nothing funny in what he had said. Still, if Mr. Blaikie wanted to laugh that was his business. Anyway who cared? For a moment he watched as the farmer turned and walked away. Then his eyes went to the small bundle of uneven fur that lay cradled in his hands. A great joy rose like a hot flame in Davie Campbell. Tenderly he poked his finger under a round, pink nose. He was rewarded a moment later when a small red tongue curled out and took a solemn lick at his finger.

'Aye,' he said huskily. 'It's plain to see you're a grand dog. A grand dog, indeed!'

Again Davie ran his fingers admiringly over the pup's body. It was strange, though, how close the ribs seemed to be against the coat; almost as if there were no flesh at all on the wee body, as if the pup had been starved. But who would ever starve a fine dog like this now? Davie dismissed the thought at once.

'I'll call you Joseph,' he said suddenly, and knew that of all names, this was the right one. For hadn't they just read last week in Sunday school about Joseph and his coat of many colours?'

'Joseph,' he said softly. 'I'm talking to you, Joseph.'

The freckled nose wrinkled. A gangling ear twitched ever so slightly. A moist brown eye winked open.

'He knows his name already,' marvelled Davie. Pride made the words tight in his throat.

from Davie's Wee Dog by W. McKellar

81. I, Too

I, too, sing America.

I am the darker brother.
They send me to eat in the kitchen
When company comes,
But I laugh,
And eat well,
And grow strong.

Tomorrow,
I'll sit at the table
When company comes.
Nobody'll dare
Say to me,
'Eat in the kitchen,'
Then.

Besides,
They'll see how beautiful I am
And be ashamed—

I, too, am America.

Langsten Hughes

82. The Broken Promise

One summer two boys and a girl went to a foster home to live together.

One of the boys was Harvey. He had two broken legs. He got them when he was run over by his father's new Grand Am.

The day of his accident was supposed to be one of the happiest of Harvey's life. He had written an essay on 'Why I am proud to be an American', and he had won third prize. Two dollars. His father had promised to drive him to the meeting and watch him get the award. The winners and their parents were going to have their pictures taken for the newspaper.

When the time came to go, Harvey's father said, 'What are you doing in the car?' Harvey had been sitting there waiting for fifteen minutes. He was wearing a tie for the first time in his life, 'Get out, Harvey, I'm late as it is.'

'Get out?'

'Yes, get out.'

Harvey did not move. He sat staring straight ahead. He said, 'But this is the night I get my award. You promised you'd take me.'

'I didn't promise. I said I would if I could.'

'No, you promised. You said if I'd quit bugging you about it, you'd take me. You promised.' He still did not look at his father.

'Get out, Harvey.'

'No.'

'I'm telling you for the last time, Harvey. Get out.'

'Drive me to the meeting and I'll get out.'

'You'll get out when I say!' Harvey's father wanted to get to a poker game at the Elk's Club and he was already late. 'And I say you get out now.' With that, the father leaned over, opened the door and pushed Harvey out of the car.

Harvey landed on his knees in the grass. He jumped to his feet. He grabbed for the car door. His father locked it.

Now Harvey looked at his father. His father's face was as red as if it had been turned inside out.

Quickly Harvey ran round the front of the car to try to open the other door. When he was directly in front of the car, his father accidentally threw the car into drive instead of reverse. In that wrong gear he pressed the accelerator, ran over Harvey and broke both his legs.

from *The Pinballs* by Betsy Byars

83. Knowing the Needs of Others

The two men sat down to eat the meal. The priest looked at the plain, sparse food in front of him and gasped with astonishment.

'What do you usually eat?' he asked the rich man.

'Oh I eat very plainly indeed,' replied the rich man. 'I have a little bread and I drink only water.'

'How ridiculous,' said the priest. 'A man of your wealth should eat the finest meat and drink fine wines. You must promise me that you will do this.'

Now it was the rich man's turn to be astonished. However he could see that the priest was quite serious so he agreed. Some time later the two met again.

'Well I am now eating meat, but why did you ask me to?'

'Ah,' said the priest, 'it is only when a rich man eats meat that he realises how much a poor man needs bread. If he eats only bread himself he thinks a poor man can live on nothing.'

84. Territory

'Forrard hoo!' yelled the sergeant. The scout with the fox fire trotted on ahead; the guidon beaver stepped out bravely under the lean banner; the troops shouldered their spears and marched off with short tails whisking, their massed black shadow keeping step with them across the moonlit snow as they herded the rations back to headquarters.

The mouse child, as he walked backwards, found himself facing the drummer boy. 'Is it really a war?' he asked the little soldier.

'Of course it is,' replied the shrew. Our territory's all hunted out, so we'll have to fight the shrews down by the stream for theirs.'

'It's the other way round, the way I heard it,' said the fifer. 'I heard their territory's all hunted out, and they invaded ours.'

'What's a territory?' asked the mouse child.

'What do you mean, "What's a territory?"' said the drummer boy. 'A territory's a territory, that's all.'

'Rations don't have territories,' said the fifer.

'Not after we catch them,' said the drummer boy, 'but they do before. Everybody does.'

'We didn't,' said the mouse child.

'No wonder you're rations now,' said the little shrew. 'What chance has anybody got without a territory?'

'But what is a territory?' asked the mouse child again.

'A territory is your place,' said the drummer boy. 'It's where everything smells right. It's where you know the runways and the hideouts, night or day. It's what you fought for, or what your father fought for, and you feel all safe and strong there. It's the place where, when you fight, you win.'

'That's your territory,' said the fifer. 'Somebody else's territory is something else again. That's where you feel all sick and scared and want to run away, and that's where the other side mostly wins.'

The father walked in silence as a wave of shame swept over him. 'What chance has anybody got without a territory?' he repeated to himself and knew the little shrew was right. What chance had they indeed! He saw now that for him and for his son the whole wide world was someone else's territory, on which he could not even walk without someone to wind him up. Frog wound him now as they marched, and the father felt the key turn in his back as a knife turns in a wound.

from *The Mouse and his Child* by Russell Hoban
(It is the story of a clockwork mouse and his father, rescued from a rubbish heap, and searching for independence.)

85. The Collier's Wife

Somebody's knockin' at th' door
  Mother, come down an' see!
—I's think it's nobbut a beggar;
  Say I'm busy.

It's not a beggar, mother; hark
  How 'ard 'e knocks!
—Eh, tha'rt a mard-arsed kid,
  'E'll gie thee socks!

Shout an' ax what 'e wants,
  I canna come down.
—'E says, is it Arthur Holliday's?
  —Say Yes, tha clown.

'E says: Tell your mother as 'er mester's
  Got hurt i' th' pit—
What? Oh my Sirs, 'e never says that,
  That's not it!

Come out o' th' way an' let me see!
  Eh, there's no peace!
An' stop they scraightin', childt,
  Do shut thy face!

'Your mester's 'ad an accident
  An' they ta'ein 'im i' th' ambulance
Ter Nottingham.'—Eh dear o' me,
  If 'e's not a man for mischance!

Wheer's 'e hurt this time, lad?
  'I dunna know,
They on'y towd me it wor bad'
  It would be so!

Out o' my way, childt! dear o' me, wheer
  'Ave I put 'is clean stockin's an' shirt?
Goodness knows if they'll be able
  To take off 'is pit dirt!

An' what a moan 'e'll make! there niver
　　Was such a man for a fuss
'If anything ailed 'im; at any rate
　　I shan't 'ave 'im to nuss.

I do 'ope as it's not so very bad!
　　Eh, what a shame it seems
As some should ha'e hardly a smite o'trouble
　　An' others 'as reams!

It's a shame as 'e should be knocked about
　　Like this, I'm sure it is!
'E's 'ad twenty accidents, if 'e's 'ad one:
　　Owt bad, an' it's his!

There's one thing, we s'll 'ave a peaceful
　　'ouse f'r a bit,
　　Thank heaven for a peaceful house!
An' there's compensation, sin' it's accident,
　　An' club money—I won't growse.

An' a fork an' spoon e'll want—an' what else?
　　I s'll never catch that train!
What a traipse it is, if a man gets hurt!
　　I sh'd think 'e'll get right again.

D.H. Lawrence

86. Courage in a Small Place

As the Imperial War Museum in London is mainly concerned with objects of war, it is rather surprising to find an ordinary old wardrobe there. This piece of furniture has no 'ordinary' story however, because it played a vital part in saving a man's life in amazing circumstances.

In 1914 a terrible battle between British and German soldiers took place at Le Cateau in France. Trooper Patrick Fowler, a British soldier, was cut off from his unit and stranded behind enemy lines. For weeks he lived on whatever scraps of food he could find and then, almost starving, he was found by a French woodcutter.

The Frenchman took Trooper Fowler to his mother-in-law's house in the village of Bertry. There he was hidden in a wardrobe until a better hiding place could be found. Before this could happen, however, eight German soldiers arrived and told Madame Belmont Gobert that they were going to live in the house!

There then followed four incredible years. With the German troops regularly moving round the house Trooper Fowler could only get out of his tiny space occasionally. When he did so he only had time for a few exercises before squeezing back into the wardrobe.

Whilst he was there Madame Belmont-Gobert faced certain death if it was discovered that she was hiding an enemy soldier. This did not seem to disturb the brave French woman who continued to help the British soldier as much as she could. The same went for the rest of the people in the village. Despite the fact that they were desperately short of food they always found Trooper Fowler something to keep him alive. Once when he was ill the local chemist risked great danger to bring him some medicine which helped a quick recovery.

Finally after four years in the wardrobe British troops returned to the village after defeating the Germans. Trooper Fowler was free! Shortly afterwards Madame Belmont-Gobert received an invitation to go to Buckingham Palace where she was awarded a medal for her great courage.

87. A World of Hunger

The year grows old and the wind
Takes on a whetted edge,
Cold without; and cold
Within my heart when I think
Of my homeland far away.

Cold are the eyes of the children there,
Hungry, full of fear.
Ragged are the children in the dust
And very hungry; here a sister
Who might have been my sister;
A brother, my brother; and scavenging
For scraps of food a mother, who
But for some quirk of fate,
Might have been my own.
A myriad mothers, sisters, brothers:
And all hungry.

The undeveloped countries is a cold phrase
With a world of hunger in it.

S. Mishra

88. Don't Look for Trouble

Kwadjo was walking through the forest one day when he heard the noise of someone singing.

'Strange,' he said to himself, 'who could that be?'

In order not to disturb the singer Kwadjo crept stealthily through the bushes towards the sound of the singing. Soon he came to a small clearing. The sound of singing was now very loud, but there was nothing to be seen.

'Whoever it is must be round here somewhere,' thought Kwadjo, 'but I can't...'

Suddenly he saw the singer, and he could hardly believe his eyes. Near a tree at the other side of the clearing, singing away at the top of his voice was—a tortoise.

As he watched and listened, exciting thoughts began to go through Kwadjo's head. A singing tortoise would be worth a fortune. All he had to do was take the creature back to the great Chief and he would never want for anything again.

Kwadjo stepped into the clearing and hurried towards the tortoise. For a moment the creature stopped singing, then it spoke.

'Good morning.'

'Not so good for you my friend,' said Kwadjo. 'You are captured and you are going to make me a fortune.'

'Oh,' replied the tortoise, 'and how am I going to do that?'

'You are coming with me and I'm going to sell you to the great Chief. Who ever heard of a singing tortoise—he will pay me a fortune to possess such a rare creature.'

'I warn you now,' said the tortoise, 'don't look for trouble. No man should do that and you will regret it if you take me from my home here.'

'Rubbish,' said Kwadjo. 'What can you do to me?'

So saying he swept the tortoise from the ground and went to the village and asked to see the Chief. As he was telling his story to the Chief, people passing by heard him and soon a large crowd had gathered round. When Kwadjo finished speaking the Chief stroked his chin and then he looked for a long time at the tortoise.

'This is a strange story,' said the Chief to Kwadjo. 'If it is true and this tortoise can indeed sing, you will have a large reward. If, however, you have tried to make a fool of me with this story then you will die instantly.'

For a moment Kwadjo felt a flicker of unease, but then he thought, 'What have I got to worry about—I've already heard this creature sing.'

Putting the tortoise on the ground he whispered to it.

'Now then, come on, sing just like you were doing in the forest.'

Silence.

Kwadjo bent closer to the tortoise and whispered more urgently.

'Sing will you!'

Silence.

Now Kwadjo was getting desperate. First he begged and pleaded with the tortoise, next he threatened it. Soon, however, the Chief got tired of this. A singing tortoise indeed. He waved his hand to two of his warriors and they seized Kwadjo and took him off to be executed.

Meanwhile the tortoise slipped away into the undergrowth. As it did so the villagers thought they heard something singing for a moment.

'Don't look for trouble . . .'

adapted from *Why the Hyena Does Not Care for Fish* by P. Appiah

89. The Gypsy

She was woken by the children clambering into her bed. At the sight of them, her wizened old face broke into a smile that accentuated the sharply etched lines between nose and chin. Her dark eyes, usually sombre, danced as she gathered them to her. Shaking back her long, dirty hair, she said, 'Well my pets did you sleep well?'

The children nodded seriously in assent. They were very much like her, with dark eyes, skin and hair; but unlike her, as their faces were plump and cherubic. She looked around the small caravan which contained all her possessions: the brass and china ornaments that sparkled now in the early morning sun, the vase that her husband had given her for their anniversary. She sighed and raised herself from the bed. Another day had begun, another day of fighting, fighting everybody, fighting for food, water, the land that she kept the caravan on, and most of all, fighting for her children. Whatever happened they must not be taken away. She cast her mind back to the day before when a man from the council had stood at the edge of the churned mud which separated her caravan from the main road and shouted: 'We give you twenty-four hours to get off this verge. It is illegal to stay here. This is council property.'

There had been threats too, from the residents of the area. They wanted no gypsies near their houses. They wanted her to go, but she could not, she had to wait until her husband returned from selling the scrap, and that would be tomorrow at the earliest. If only they would all stay away for just one more day, surely they could leave her alone for that long? What had she done to be so cruelly treated?

The day wore on. They had only one stale loaf between the three of them; she had no fuel to make a fire, no water to boil, nothing to feed the children with. The expression of hunger and unhappiness in their eyes hurt her more than anything else; they trusted her and she could do nothing to help them.

It was late afternoon when a man, followed by a group of people approached the caravan . . .

Angela Goddard, aged 16

90. 'Why Doesn't Somebody Do Something?'

In Jerusalem the people were dissatisfied,
Nothing was as it should be.
Roman soldiers stalked the streets
Having it all their own way.
Taxes were too high and the gatherers were cheats,
The government didn't seem to care,
And Pontius Pilate—well, why should he bother?

'Never Mind,' they said—
'Somebody will be along soon,
Somebody to put it all right . . .
Somebody to show the Romans where to get off
And make us free again.'

Just then a carpenter turned up,
A Northerner who talked good sense,
A practical man who practised what he preached.
'I am the Way,' he said, 'but you will have to tread the path for yourself.'

The people listened, some of them,
Others heard, but they did not like what they heard.
'It's all very well for him to talk,' they said,
'Why doesn't he strike down Pilate with a thunderbolt?
Fancy asking us to get up and do something about it!
We are looking for a Saviour, not a Do-It-Yourself merchant.'
And they settled themselves down for a good grumble,
Most of them.

So when the Romans came, and took him in the night,
Most of them looked the other way—
And while he hung dying they shook their heads—
'Serves him right for asking us to do something about it.'

After it was all over,
And a few who said he was alive again had apparently disappeared,
The Roman soldiers stalked the streets,
And the people of Jerusalem were dissatisfied.

Claude Holmes

91. Learning

Willie is a small boy who has been evacuated from his home in London during the Second World War. He knows nothing at all about the country and has been regularly and badly beaten by his mother. When he reaches a village in the country he is told he has to live with Tom, an old widower. Tom goes out and Willie wanders out of the cottage to look around outside . . .

'Sniffing and scratching among the leaves at the foot of the tree was a squirrel. He recognised its shape from pictures he had seen but he wasn't prepared for one that moved. He was terrified and remained frozen in a crouched position. The squirrel seemed quite unperturbed and carried on scuffling about in the leaves, picking up nuts and tit-bits in its tiny paws. Willie stayed motionless, hardly breathing. He felt like the stone angel. The squirrel's black eyes darted in a lively manner from place to place. It was tiny, light grey in colour with a bushy tail that stuck wildly in the air as it poked its paws and head into the russet and gold leaves.

After a while Willie's shoulders relaxed and the gripping sensation in his stomach subsided a little. He wriggled his toes gingerly inside his plimsolls. It seemed as though he had been crouching for hours although it couldn't have been more than ten minutes.

The little fellow didn't seem to scare him as much, and he began to enjoy watching him. A loud sharp barking suddenly disturbed the silence. The squirrel leapt and disappeared. Willie sprang to his feet, hopping on one leg and gasping at the mixture of numbness and pins and needles in the other. A small black-and-white collie ran around the tree and into the leaves. It stopped in front of him and jumped up into the air. Willie was more petrified of the dog than he had been of the squirrel.

"Them poisonous dogs," he heard his mother's voice saying inside him. "One bite from them muts and you're dead. They got 'orrible diseases in 'em." He remembered the tiny children's graves and quickly picked up a thick branch from the ground.

"You go away," he said feebly, gripping it firmly in his hand. "You go away."

The dog sprang into the air again and barked and yapped at him, tossing leaves by his legs. Willie let out a shriek and drew back. The dog came nearer.

"I'll kill you."

"I wouldn't do that," said a deep voice behind him. He turned to find Tom standing by the outer branches. "He ent goin' to do you no 'arm, so I should jest drop that if I was you."

Willie froze with the branch still held high in his hand. Sweat broke out from under his armpits and across his forehead. Now he was for it. He was bound to get a beating now. Tom came towards him, took the branch firmly from his hand and lifted it up. Willie automatically flung his arm across his face and gave a cry but the blow he was expecting never came. Tom had merely thrown the branch to the other end of the graveyard and the dog had gone scampering after it.

"You can take yer arm down now boy," he said quietly. "I think you and I 'ad better go inside and sort a few things out. Come on," and with that he stepped aside for Willie to go in front of him along the path.'

from *Goodnight Mister Tom* by Michelle Magorian

92. Under the Hazy, Blossom-laden Sky

Under the hazy, blossom-laden sky
The city sprawls, its gaping wounds exposed:
The streets due for a surgical operation,
Canals gathering pitch and filth,
Bridges with their concrete peeling away.

Under the hazy, blossom-laden sky
Cranes moving,
Drain-pipes lined up,
Truck after truck
Carrying dirt, rubbish, mud,
The burnt-out, festering hulks of war.

Dark caverns in the streets:
On the canal bed, submerged groans and sighs
Of those who will not surface:
Methane gushing up.

In the city with those clogged wounds
International streets will appear soon,
Rows of gay shops will grow,
Tempting goods will brighten the windows.

Under the hazy, blossom-laden sky
New building goes on.
Our ears tuned to the detonations under the hazy, blossom-laden sky,
We pray
That the fire-rain never again falls on the world.

Okamoto Jun

93. Look beneath the Surface

Imagine that you have a small, mishappen body; your face is a strange, twisted shape and you cannot speak properly because you have a terrible stammer. On top of this imagine that you are a slave who lived nearly three thousand years ago. Your master could decide in an instant whether you lived or died and you could spend your life being treated like an animal.

Although we don't know many facts about him it seems that this is how Aesop, one of the world's greatest 'tellers of tales' began his life. Those people who looked at him and laughed or treated him with contempt soon learned, however, what a quick and intelligent mind hid behind his appearance. He proved this one day when he and his fellow slaves were given orders to carry goods to a nearby market.

'Every slave will carry a weight equal to his strength,' said the merchant in charge, 'that means you needn't carry anything Aesop!'

There was a great laugh from the other slaves at this but Aesop, whose stammer was now almost cured, replied calmly as if no joke had been made about him.

'No master, that would not be fair,' he replied. 'I will carry the bread basket.'

At this there was another roar of laughter. The bread basket was the heaviest thing of all which had to be carried.

'Not only is he ugly, he's stupid as well,' muttered one of the slaves.

'He certainly is,' replied another.

So the great line of men set off. Each bent under the weight of his burden until the call came to stop and eat. At once the master called out:

'Give every man his bread ration.'

So Aesop's basket was emptied, and when the journey was continued after the stop his burden was the lightest of all. As the slaves marched on their comments were rather different.

'He's no fool that Aesop is he?'

'No—he knew what he was doing when he chose that basket.'

'Just shows—it doesn't do to judge people too quickly.'

adapted from La Fontaine

94. Home Thoughts from Home

The sunlight is pierced with screams
and gurgling laughter and the endless
splash of water as small boys
shiny black as seals,
catapult, head over heels,
into the warm blue sea . . .
Yes, I am truly home—back again on my
birth-island: sun on sea, sighing coconut-tree,
shrill cry of the Keskidee. And yet,
I do nothing but lie here and fret!

Oh, to be in England, now that autumn's there
in London—but most happily in Hampstead,
where, a score of sycamores have shed a ton of
red-brown leaves on the narrow street that
climbs away, up from Holly Hill. But still, I
would rather wade, ankle-deep, in dead leaves
than walk gingerly now on sun-hot sand. Or have
the Heath reach out a chill hand to clap my shoulder
in rude warning, of winter rigours yet to come.
And watch, by the hour, the pale
ghost water of Whitestone Pond rippled by an
unseen gale . . .

. . . And if you should fail
to understand why I can think only of England,
lying on Tobago's sand, then *you* have never known
the exquisite ache of loving two islands—
that if from one you roam, you can only think
constantly of the other. Thinking always,
home thoughts from home!

Rick Ferreira

95.   A Likely Story

The two men were out hunting.

'Let's prepare our traps and then go home for supper,' said Si Kebayan.

'That's a good idea,' said his father-in-law. 'What are you going to try and catch?'

'I want something with plenty of meat on it so it will feed many people,' said Si Kebayan. 'I am going to dig a deep hole so that I might catch a deer.'

'Oh that sounds like very hard work to me. I'm just going to put a trap in a tree in the hope that I can catch a bird or two.'

So the two men set their traps. It took Si Kebayan much longer to prepare his and he was very tired when he got home. Meanwhile his father-in-law had done very little so he got up at sunrise the next morning and returned to the traps. Sure enough there was a deer in Si Kebayan's trap—and nothing in his own.

'We'll soon put this right,' said the father-in-law, dragging the deer from the pit and forcing it into the bird trap.

He then went home and got back into bed. A few minutes later Si Kebayan came by.

'Come on,' he shouted, 'time to get up and see what we have caught.'

'Oh, ah,' yawned the father-in-law, pretending that he had just woken up. 'Is it morning already?'

Soon the two men came to the traps. The father-in-law looked up and shouted, 'Good, look what I have got!'

Si Kebayan looked up at the deer in his father-in-law's trap then he looked in his own and saw all the footprints and damage round.

The father-in-law began boasting.

'Ah well, better luck next time Si Kebayan. I'm afraid I'm very hungry so don't expect any meat from me. You'll just have to wait until you catch something in your own trap.'

As he spoke he noticed that Si Kebayan was looking up at the sky.

'What are you looking for?' asked the father-in-law.

'Fish'.

'Fish! You must be mad. Whoever heard of fish flying about in the sky?'

'The same person who might have heard of deer flying about in the sky.'

When Si Kebayan said this the father-in-law knew that his selfish trick had been discovered and he was ashamed. He apologised to Si Kebayan who was kind enough to let him share the meat of the deer.

adapted from *Folk Tales of Indonesia* by A. Soebiantoro and M. Ratnatunga

96. Think Twice

The king was very sad. His mother was sick. She was so sick that everybody was sure she would die.

'There is only one person who might be able to help,' thought the king. He called to one of his men.

'Bring Ananse the Spider here. He is the cleverest creature we know in Ghana. He might be able to help my mother.'

Ananse was brought before the king. He listened carefully and then he spoke.

'I will give you some medicine for your mother Oh King—but if she is so sick she may still die. I must warn you of this.'

'The medicine, the medicine,' cried the king impatiently.

So the king gave his mother Ananse's medicine. Because he had heard the spider was so clever he was sure that his mother would soon get well. But the old lady was too ill and in a few days time she died.

When the king got over being very very sad at the death of his mother he suddenly thought to himself:

'Hmmm. Ananse is supposed to be so clever. And I paid him gold for that medicine. He did nothing to save my mother. He must die!'

Well, when Ananse heard that the king's mother had died he was sure that it would be only a matter of time before the king's men came for him. So he made some plans.

He asked one of his animal friends to dig a tunnel under the ground. This tunnel went right under the spot where the king had his throne. Next he got a horn from the man who made horns and drums. He dragged the horn into the tunnel. Then he spoke to his son.

'Now listen Son,' said Ananse. 'When he gets over the sadness of his mother's death the king is sure to blame me because my medicine couldn't save her life. When the soldiers come to take me away I want you to crawl into that horn and when you hear what is going on above, this is what I want you to shout . . .'

'But . . .' began Ananse's son.

'Don't worry,' said Ananse. 'Just do as I've told you.'

No sooner had Ananse finished his preparations than the king's men came for him. Soon he found himself standing in front of the angry king.

'You're not so wise, Ananse' said the king. 'Your medicine didn't work and my mother is dead so—you must die!'

No sooner had the king spoken than a strange voice boomed out. It seemed to come from right under the ground beneath the king's throne.

'Kill Ananse and all will weep', cried the voice.

Everybody round about heard the voice and they were very frightened. Then it spoke again.

'Spare Ananse and all will laugh,' it said.

Now the king was very frightened too. He thought the voice must belong to some spirit. Trying not to look frightened he stroked his chin, and then spoke aloud to his people.

'My mother is dead,' he said. 'Killing Ananse will not bring her back. The last thing I want is for my people to be unhappy and weep.'

Then he turned to his soldiers who were holding Ananse.

'Release him,' he said to them. 'Ananse, you are free to go.'

97. Christmas Day

There was a certain Christmas Day, about forty-five years ago. Among my presents that morning were a football and a red-and-white striped football shirt. I put on the shirt and took the football out to the nearest field, which was, I distinctly remember, covered with snow (We always had snow for Christmas when I was a boy). It was a leaden morning, with the weight of a dozen sullen Sundays pressing upon it; but round and round that field I went, kicking my beautiful football, now dribbling along the wing past four or five imaginary opponents, now dashing in towards invisible posts and nets to score tremendous goals. I was as solitary as Robinson Crusoe, and quite happy, grandly conscious of myself in my red-and-white stripes. Then, in the afternoon, when parents and relatives, somnolent after the huge Christmas dinner of that time, were muttering and snoring and no use to a boy, I went to play with the boy next door. He had been given an angry little engine that worked a miniature printing press. All that it could print were two smudgy ducks, but they were good enough for my friend and me. After collecting every bit of waste-paper in the house, we spent hours keeping the engine going and printing hundreds and hundreds of ducks, smudgier and smudgier ducks. It was a day of pure delight, and I could not buy one like it now for a thousand pounds.

from *Delight* by J.B. Priestley

98. What Do You See?

One day Toshiro was walking along a lovely path near his home. Suddenly he saw the sun glinting off something which lay on the ground just ahead of him. He picked it up and gasped in astonishment.

Now what Toshiro had picked up was a pocket mirror. However, he had never seen a mirror before as there were none in this part of Japan at the time. When Toshiro looked in the mirror therefore he thought he was seeing the picture of a face.

'It's my father,' he thought. 'What is a picture of my father doing lying here on this path?'

Toshiro couldn't think of an answer to this question so he took the mirror home with him. His wife was out when he got home and he put the mirror behind a large vase.

'Now I can remind myself of my dear father anytime I want to,' he thought. 'All I've got to do is get his picture down.'

A few days later Toshiro's wife was cleaning the house. First she dusted round the large vase and as her hand went behind it she touched something which had not been there before.

'I wonder what this can be?' she said to herself as she lifted the mirror out.

She looked into it, and then cried out in anger and disappointment.

'It's a woman!' she said aloud. 'All the years Toshiro and I have been married—and now he is hiding a picture of another woman in the house!'

That night Toshiro and his wife had a terrible argument about the 'picture'. It was so loud that the local priest who was passing by heard the shouting and came into the house.

'Friends, friends,' he cried, 'whatever is the matter. This is not like you. What is the trouble?'

First the tearful wife put her side of the story. Then her bewildered husband told the priest about how he had found the mirror.

'Well,' said the priest, 'perhaps the best thing to do is to let me see this picture which has caused all the trouble.'

Toshiro brought the mirror. The priest looked into it. 'Why should this cause you to argue?' he asked. 'This is no picture of an old man or a woman with a wicked face. It is the picture of a kind, thoughtful man. I will take it with me and put it in a place of honour in the temple.'

So saying the priest took the mirror, and Toshiro and his wife lived peacefully again.

99. A Man of His Word

The Muslims were saying their dawn prayers and Nasrudin was praying loudly.

'Allah, please send me one hundred gold pieces. I promise that if you only send me ninety-nine I will not have them.'

A very rich merchant lived near Nasrudin and he heard this prayer.

'Aha,' thought the merchant, 'I'll bet it's easy to make Nasrudin break his word.' Having thought this he collected up ninety-nine pieces of gold and put them in a bag. Then he left the bag by Nasrudin's house.

Sure enough Nasrudin found it almost immediately. Opening the bag he carefully counted out ninety-nine pieces of gold, smiled, and then spoke aloud.

'Allah has sent me ninety-nine pieces of gold—I'm sure he will see that I get the other one to make up a hundred very shortly.'

Now whilst Nasrudin had been counting the gold the merchant was watching from a secret hiding place. When he heard Nasrudin say this he suddenly got worried. If this silly man was going to wait for the other gold piece to arrive—when was he going to get his money back? There was only one thing to do. That night he went to Nasrudin and told him all about the trick.

'A joke . . . a joke!' said Nasrudin as he listened. 'My friend there is no joke. Allah has sent me ninety-nine coins and I am waiting for the hundredth. This money is mine—not yours.'

The merchant was furious when he heard this.

'Right, we must go to the Cadi and get his judgement on this,' he said.

Now it was a long journey to the Cadi's court. Nasrudin said he certainly wanted to go and have justice done. But he was an old man—could the merchant lend him a donkey to ride on, and a better coat to wear than the tattered old jubbeh which was the only coat he had?

Angrily the merchant agreed to this and the two men eventually arrived at the Cadi's court. Immediately the merchant told his story and demanded his money back.

The Cadi looked àt Nasrudin who had stood silently through all this.

'What have you got to say?' asked the Cadi.

'Well, Effendi,' said Nasrudin. 'I asked Allah for gold coins and sure enough they came to me. This man is my neighbour and he must have watched me counting the coins and is now trying to trick me out of what is mine.'

At this the merchant was furious.

'I put the coins by this man's house—because I knew he would never keep his word to return them unless there was one hundred!'

'Ha!' said Nasrudin, 'what stories you tell my friend. Next you will be saying that my clothes are yours—and even the donkey I rode here on!'

The merchant grew purple with rage. 'They are . . . they are mine . . . you know that perfectly well you . . . !'

At this point the Cadi interrupted.

'Stop!' he shouted. Then he turned to the merchant.

'First you accuse a man of having your money. Then you say he has your clothes—and donkey as well. That is too much. Be off with you. Nasrudin the money is yours.'

When the two men got outside the court the merchant couldn't believe what had happened. He just stood there, miserable and confused.

Then Nasrudin patted him on the shoulder.

'Come my friend,' he said. 'I know the money is yours. Come to my house for a meal and then I will give you it all back—and the coat and the donkey. But remember this—never try to get a good Muslim to break his word again!'

100. It Is Better to Help Than to Destroy

A king was once worried about all the many decisions he had to make in his kingdom.

'Ah,' he thought to himself, 'I must decide about so many things, who is right here, who is right there. If only I could see the Great Prophet and get his advice how much easier life would be. In fact if anybody could find the Great Prophet for me I would give him great riches.'

Now many people heard this and, the next day, a poorly dressed man appeared at the palace.

'Your majesty, if you will pay me the reward I will help you to see the Great Prophet.'

'Hm,' said the king, 'how do I know you can make this happen?'

'Well,' said the man, 'give me forty days. If I cannot get the Great Prophet to see you within forty days, you may have me executed.'

The king agreed to the bargain and the man was paid a large sum of money. As soon as he got it he went straight home. There he bought his wife and children the best meal they had had in years. Then he bought the first decent clothes they had ever had. Next he paid of his debts and made sure that his family would want for nothing for a very long time.

Then he went back to see the king.

'Your majesty,' he said, 'I have come to confess. I am just a very poor man. I was at my wit's end as to how to care for my family when I heard your promise. I am sorry I have tricked you. I cannot bring the Great Prophet to you—so you must execute me as you will.'

The king listened to this carefully. At first he was furious, then he got worried again.

'More decisions,' he thought to himself irritably. 'I'll have to consult my ministers.'

So he told his three chief ministers the story and asked their advice.

'Kill the scoundrel,' said the first minister.

'He must certainly die,' said the second.

'What treachery he has shown,' said the third. 'He must be executed for not keeping his part of the bargain.'

The king was just about to pass judgement when he saw an old, grey haired man standing near a pillar. The man had a very wise, calm face and in desperation the king spoke to him.

'I suppose you think the same?' he said.

At once the old man answered in a quiet, thoughtful voice.

'No. Your ministers have advised you wrongly. If you kill this man you will have achieved nothing. Really he is a good man who was prepared to give up his life for the well-being of his wife and family. If you forgive him you will never have a more loyal subject and he will never stop telling others of your wisdom and mercy.'

'You're right,' said the king as soon as he heard this. 'You're absolutely right. Now . . .'

He turned to speak to the old man again but he had disappeared as suddenly as he had come.

'The Great Prophet,' murmured the king. He then freed the poor man who had tricked him, sent his ministers off to ports far away and ruled for the rest of his life with a wisdom which made him famous.

adapted from *Folk Tales of Iran* by A. Dhar

101. Jamaican Night Meeting

Sometimes our imagination makes us frightened when there is no need to be—and this is particularly so when we are alone and in a strange place. This is the story of Ranny, whose car broke down on a Jamaican road one night.

Realising that he couldn't get the car to go himself Ranny set off to walk along the road to the nearest village. There was nobody about because it was a dreadful night. Shafts of lightning flashed across the sky and thunder growled ominously every few minutes. Ranny walked along the road listening to his footsteps and the strange night sounds around him. Then he heard the long, sad screech of an owl.

At once he felt nervous for he remembered the long ago stories of his childhood which said that the night cry of an owl meant ill luck for those who heard it. Then he remembered how this bad luck could be stopped—if you shouted aloud the correct words.

'What were those words?' thought Ranny as he walked nervously on. 'Ah, yes, now I know.'

The owl screeched again and without stopping walking Ranny threw back his head and yelled at the top of his voice:

'Salt an' pepper fe yo mumma!'

At once two things happened: the owl stopped its screeching, but just in front of Ranny there was a cry of terror. He just had time to see an enormous shape towering over him, and then it crashed off, leaving the road and pounding through a canefield, snapping and smashing through the crop.

When Ranny eventually reached the village he spent the night there. Next morning he got up early to see about his car.

As he was walking through the village square he saw that a little crowd was gathered there. Standing in front of them was an enormous man and he was telling them . . .

'. . . so never go along that road at night. I tell you it's haunted. There I was, walking along, when suddenly this creature appeared in front of me. What a size it was! Then when it was almost up to me it let out this terrible roar—I tell you I jumped off that road and I didn't stop running until I was back in my own house with the door locked and bolted top and bottom!'

102.　To Give and to Receive

Leon was sitting at home one day. Everyone else was out of the house. He was just finishing his dinner when there was a knock at the door. When Leon answered the knock he saw a beggar standing on his doorstep.

'Please,' said the beggar, 'could you spare me a little money so that I can buy some food.'

'Yes, of course,' said Leon and went inside to the drawer where his wife kept the money. When he opened it however he found that she had taken it all out shopping with her. Putting his hands into his pockets he found that he had no money either.

Feeling rather embarrassed Leon was on his way back to the door when he noticed one of the vases which stood on the mantelpiece.

'That must be worth something,' he thought to himself.

Picking it up he returned to where the beggar was waiting and gave him the vase.

'I'm sorry I have no money,' said Leon, 'but this vase should be worth a little if you sell it.'

'Oh,' said the beggar, looking a little disappointed. 'Well, thank you very much anyway.'

A little while later Leon's wife returned. When she noticed the vase was missing and heard the story she was furious.

'Don't you know that vase was worth a great deal of money? How stupid of you. Fancy giving away something as valuable as that—what are you going to do about it?'

'I must do something at once,' replied Leon, picking up his coat and hurrying out.

He caught up with the beggar before the man had got into town. He was still carrying the vase, dangling from his left hand.

'Stop! Stop!' shouted Leon.

The beggar stopped and looked round as Leon came hurrying towards him.

'That vase,' gasped Leon breathlessly, 'apparently it is worth far more than I thought. When you sell it make sure that you get a good price and are not cheated.'

Acknowledgements

For permission to reproduce copyright material the author and publisher are indebted to the following:

2. 'If', Charlie Savvides, from *Hot Dogs*, Tollington Park School, Turle Road, London N4 3LS
40. *The Black Gull of Corrie Lachan*, M. MacAlpine, Faber and Faber
42. 'A Cat' from *Selected Poems* by Edward Thomas, Faber and Faber and Myfanwy Thomas
45. 'Silent, But . . .' Tsuboi Shigeji, trans. G. Bownas and A. Thwaite, *Penguin Book of Japanese Verse*, Penguin
48. 'A Play-mate's Doom', Philip Leighton, *Word Spinning*, ed. F. Clement, Evans
50. 'Easter', Monica Furlong and Anthony Sheil Associates
78. 'A Stranger', Katerina Theoharous, from *Hot Dogs*, Tollington Park School
80. *Davie's Wee Dog*, W. McKellar, Bodley Head
81. 'I Too', Langsten Hughes, *The Illustrated Treasury of Poetry for Children*, ed. D. Ross, William Collins
82. *The Pinballs*, Betsy Byars, Bodley Head
84. *The Mouse and his Child*, Russell Hoban, Faber and Faber
87. 'A World of Hunger', S. Mishra, from *There's Rosemary*, Gwent Education Committee
89. 'The Gypsy', Angela Goddard, from *Hertfordshire Children's Writing No. 6*, Herts. Education Committee
90. 'Why Doesn't Somebody Do Something?', Claude Holmes, from *Together*, Church Information Office
91. *Goodnight Mister Tom*, Michelle Magorian, Kestrel
92. 'Under the Hazy, Blossom-laden Sky', Okamoto Jun, from *Penguin Book of Japanese Verse*
94. 'Home Thoughts from Home', Rick Ferreira, *How Strong the Roots*, ed. H. Sergeant, Evans
97. 'Christmas Day', J.B. Priestley, *Delight*, Heinemann

The author and publisher would also like to acknowledge the following sources of adapted stories:

1., 23. adapted from *Folk Tales of Thailand*, P.C.R. Chandur, Sterling
3., 95. adapted from *Folk Tales of Indonesia*, A. Soebiantoro and M. Ratnatunga, Sterling
5., 63. adapted from *The Caravan of Dreams*, Idris Shah, Octagon Press
7. adapted from *The Ivory City*, M. Crouch, Granada
10. adapted from material broadcast on B.B.C. Playhouse, November 1970
11., 100. adapted from *Folk Tales of Iran*, A. Dhar, Sterling
14. adapted from *Stories Told round the World*, T. Zinkin, O.U.P.
19. adapted from *The Epic of Gilgamesh*, N.K. Sanders, Penguin
26. adapted from *Dragons, Gods and Spirits from Chinese Mythology*, T.T.L. Sanders, Peter Lowe
28., 64. adapted from *Folk Tales of Sri Lanka*, M. Ratnatunga, Sterling
46. adapted from *A Second Storyteller's Choice*, E. Colwell, Bodley Head
57. adapted from *Folk Tales of Turkey*, S. Dhar, Sterling
68., 69., 72. adapted from *Village Folk Tales of Ceylon*, H. Parker, Tisara Press
74. adapted from *The Magic Book of Birds*, T. Haddon, Canongate
88. adapted from *Why the Hyena does Not Care for Fish*, P. Appiah, Andre Deutsch
101. adapted from original material from the Jamaican High Commission

For permission to reproduce the cover photographs the author and publisher are indebted to the following:

Richard & Sally Greenhill; bottom left
Alan Hutchison Library; bottom left and top left
MEPhA; top right